A.B.Normal
Publishing and Media Group
Anything but normal.

A.B.Normal Publishing and Media Group
PO Box 31311
Knoxville, TN 37930
www.abnormalpublishing.com

Publisher's note: The story, all names, characters, and incidents portrayed in this production are fictitious. No identification with actual persons (living or deceased), places, buildings, and products is intended or should be inferred.

Library of Congress Control Number: 2020949205

Hardcover ISBN: 978-1-7350597-0-9

Paperback ISBN: 978-0-9983930-8-7

Kindle ASIN: B089ZYFV99

Edited by Rachel Small. Title card logo design by Chuck Regan.

Cover art and design by Rock_0407002E.

Requiem for Lilith / Robert J. McCartney & Albert J. Debusschere III — Revised First Print 2025

CONTENTS

To my wife and kids.
My parents.
Thanks, Al. Sorry, I mean, Joe. ;)

To the members of Morphine (Mark Sandman, Dana Colley, Jerome Deupree, Billy Conway) for the inspiration and for helping me find myself after our car accident through your music.

I want to expand on this and also include Treat Her Right, Hypnosonics, Vapors of Morphine, and so on.

"You can be anything you want to be, despite what other people may say. My advice is this: be anything but normal."
Robert J. McCartney

Read Book Two in the Willborne Saga *Lilah's Guide to Hoyle*, available along with other titles.

Visit www.abnormalpublishing.com for free stories, information, and more.

Scan this QR code for
Lilah's Guide to Hoyle

A Note from the Author
Boop

When I first wrote *Requiem for Lilith*, *Lilah's Guide to Hoyle* (and the original *Bob*), I had a vision of how the pieces would fall into place. Returning to these stories years later, revising and reshaping them, I've adjusted the endgame and added new layers. I believe the result is stronger—more aligned with what I had always hoped to create.

The flow remains familiar, but there's new content woven throughout. Like *Bob*, certain roles are a little clearer, others are teased, and the stage is set for a saga that I hope is as engaging in its whole as it is in its parts.

My goal has always been to make each story stand on its own—relatable, shareable, and open enough that you can step in at any point and still understand where you are. That said, some connections and details will only fully reveal themselves over time. I trust you'll enjoy the changes and additions, and I invite you to join me on the long road to the end.

Use that free will.

Until next time,
RJM

P.S. You've been booped.

PROLOGUE

)

The Song Yet Unsung

THE WORLD HUMS WITH quiet anticipation, though no one hears it. A line of shadows moves across its surface—broken, beautiful, fracturing in the light. Pieces shift before they know the rules. Moves are made in whispers, glances, breaths held too long.

A song rises somewhere in the distance, faint, almost forgotten, its notes threading through the air like currents unseen. It carries loss, love, the stirring of things not yet born. The melody bends the world, and she does not know. Each tone a spark, each refrain a whisper of battles yet to come.

She sings for hope she barely trusts, for love she fears will betray her, for loss that has already begun to take root.

The board is set. Some pieces will move freely; others will be forced. The gambit stretches beyond sight, across time, across hearts, across the spaces where the living and the shadowed collide.

The rhythm of the unseen hand marks every step. The song is both a warning and a herald, quiet yet unstoppable. It shapes the battlefield even as it lingers in silence. Every heartbeat, every choice, every fear spins threads unseen, binding friend to foe, brother to sister, hunter to prey.

Love and loss entwine—hope and despair dance. The melody rises, inevitable, and she carries it unaware, her song a trumpet for the war to come.

And I—

I will record it all: every note, every silence, every shadowed movement of the pieces yet to fall.

The war has begun.

The song will be sung.

Now . . .

We begin.

CHAPTER 1

OUT OF BREATH, LYNALY hopped into the passenger seat of Sam's small black coupe. "I'm sorry. I didn't mean to keep you waiting! I couldn't find my purse."

Her boyfriend's bright blue eyes shone as he leaned over the center console to kiss her. "It's OK, we'll make it."

"It's just that we've been planning this for weeks, and something always pops up," she said. "It's like some force is keeping us from the place."

The pair had an unnatural attraction to each other. Childhood sweethearts, they often joked that they were lovers from another time, fated to be together forever. There was nothing that one did without the other. And now that they were eighteen, Sam had plans for them both beyond school.

Sam jerked the car into gear and pulled away from Lynaly's parents' house. It was small, well-kept, and unremarkable in a quiet neighborhood. Lynaly glanced out the window at the kids playing in her neighbors' yards. The sun warmed her face, and she smiled, enjoying the sensation, before returning to Sam. "Are you still having the dreams?"

He nodded. "Yeah, they've been pretty frequent this week."

"At first, they had been sporadic," he told her. In the dreams, he fought men dressed in ornate armor and killed for God during the Crusades. His dream self also encountered a woman who looked like Lynaly and sought to learn magic. Eventually, he renounced his knighthood and practiced magic in secret. Together, he and the woman had grand plans to improve the world—until he was murdered.

"Last night, I had the dream where my best friend killed me," he said.

"Did you see his face?"

Sam shook his head with a sigh. "It's always obscured like he had a mask on, or I was never meant to see it."

Glancing at the dashboard clock, Lynaly frowned. "Are you sure we'll make it? It's about quarter to."

"Yeah, we'll make it." He peered at the approaching street signs. "Hang on, I know a shortcut."

He jerked the wheel, making an abrupt left turn. Lynaly clung to the small bar on the roof near the door as Sam sped down a side street and glided through several intersections.

Lynaly's heart raced. "Be careful, Sam."

"Yeah, yeah, don't worry, babe," he said, approaching another intersection. "Just past this light, and we're there!" He looked over at Lynaly and smiled.

She returned the smile as Sam slowed to a halt at the red light. Almost immediately, the light flickered to green. Sam peered both ways. All was still. Only as he accelerated into the intersection did the red blur with golden eyes make itself known, rapidly approaching from his left. There was a monstrous roar. Sam's eyes widened, but no sound escaped his open mouth. It was as if his voice had been stripped from his body.

An ear-shattering shriek. Crunching metal and bone. The smell of rubber.

The red beast lay battered, broken—its pieces strewn across the black asphalt like a jigsaw puzzle. The blood of its occupants sprinkled the intersection.

Amid the wreckage, Sam lay still, his eyes open, bloodied tears streaking down his cheeks. Blood poured from his mouth over his motionless chest. His shoulder blade protruded through what was once the driver's window. His head hung loose, facing Lynaly.

It wasn't until people started shouting, offering aid, and notifying emergency services that Lynaly opened her eyes. She couldn't understand what she saw through her blurred and distorted vision. She blinked several times, attempting to regain focus.

Sharp pain pulsed through her body. Her legs were cold, but warmth saturated her chest. Her vision cleared momentarily, and she saw Sam—contorted, broken, lifeless. She tried to call out for him but could only gurgle through the blood.

In her mind, she heard Sam's voice. "*I'm sorry, Lynaly.*"

Tears streamed down her cheeks. "Samael . . . don't leave me . . . no . . . please."

"*The book, Lynaly.*"

The words echoed in her mind, eternally, it seemed, as darkness enveloped her.

Then she heard a soft voice. It was mostly incoherent, but Lynaly could make out one thing: it was offering her help.

)

All around her was the night. A tiny blue spark of life shimmered before her in the endless sea of blackness. Then, the ghostly presence rearranged itself into Sam. Lynaly's arms felt heavy as she reached out to touch him. The light projected by his body illuminated the dark prison that confined her.

He smiled at her and spoke softly, his voice echoing. "I'm waiting for you, Lynaly."

Gray mist penetrated the darkness all around her. Warm streams ran down Lynaly's cheeks as she gazed upon the translucent Sam. Suddenly, the darkness lifted. A full moon nestled within the makeshift heavens, offering a pale glow illuminating the crimson sea where she bathed. Spotting a small island, she crawled onto it. Sam had disappeared; in his place, a new face manifested. It knew her. It knew her all too well.

The gray mist absorbed the red sea and offered a woman's curves: the Lady of the Night. She stood tall in all her elegant, seductive splendor. Green-gray eyes sat on her face, clear of impurities and imperfections. Her hair was white with wisdom, and her satin skin was as pure as the moon's glow. In her headband was a bright crimson garnet resembling a Solomon protection seal in the middle of her forehead. She wore a white gown that hugged her hips and full bosom, and its sleeves draped low, suggesting wings. Her full lips were painted black like the night.

"Lynaly, I am all too familiar with the pains of love, of having it pried from you by death's icy grasp. For you see,

I was once like you. I enjoyed everything life offered, only to watch it be torn asunder. My love was taken and slain before my eyes."

The shade knelt before Lynaly, her eyes offering compassion. Lynaly's uneasiness dissipated as she stared into the depths of the shade's gaze and saw a past event take shape: A beautiful woman, restrained in chain shackles, watched in horror as two men, who appeared as phantoms, held a battered man whose face she couldn't see. Then, a third phantom branded the victim a traitor with a hot wrought-iron cross.

"Your sins shall not go unpunished, traitor of the cross!" one of the phantoms said. "May you suffer in the depths of Hell, heathen!" He then raised his holy sword and thrust the blade deep into the man's abdomen. Blood sprayed the ground. The man never screamed, never cried—only looked on his love as he collapsed, waiting for the specter of death to usher him to Hell.

Each phantom took hold of a woman's limb bound in chains. Labeling her a heathen, a witch, and a demon, they carried her to a pit of fire, and after slitting limbs, they cast her into it. As the flames proceeded to consume her, she screamed a bloody vengeance and cursed at the phantoms.

Lynaly snapped back to the present darkness. The shade closed her eyes and turned away.

"So, now, you have seen what happened. You, dear child, are still alive, and I am no longer there. You can bring back your love through the mystic magic I was given long ago." The shade met Lynaly's gaze again and offered her hand. "However, know that there is a price—"

"How? Where do I get this magic of yours?"

The shade grinned. "Kerouac's Relics and Antiquities."

Lynaly frowned. "That's where—"

"Yes, where you and Sam were going to obtain the rings he had inquired about."

"Yes, how did you know?"

The shade smiled again. "I was like you, Lynaly. In many ways, you are me, and I am you."

Lynaly smiled. "Sam and I loved magic and its history, especially witchcraft." She dropped her head. "If you are certain it will work, I'll do it and go to Kerouac's. I don't care what it costs or what it will take. I cannot be without Sam—I may as well be dead!"

"There, there, child. I will help. Trust in me." The majestic shade knelt beside Lynaly and placed a hand on her shoulder.

Lynaly gazed upon the beauty of the night. "What is your name?"

"You can call me Lilly, my dear."

)

Slowly, Lynaly opened her heavy eyes. Two familiar faces greeted her.

"Mom? Dad?" she said weakly.

"It's OK, sweetie, we're right here," her mother said soothingly. She grasped her hand and began weeping.

Lynaly tried to take in her surroundings. She appeared in a hospital bed, and the bright sun bathed the ghostly white room.

"Mona, come now, she's just woken up," Lynaly's father said sternly. "Don't crowd her too much. Not even one minute, and you're practically suffocating the poor girl."

Mona frowned. "I'm simply concerned about our daughter, Johnny."

Johnny smiled and looked down at Lynaly. "Your mother looks so cute when she makes that squiggle with her brow, don't you think?" he said, attempting to lighten the mood.

Mona was a short, petite woman. Lynaly had inherited her vibrant green eyes and long golden hair but was taller and had long legs.

Lynaly continued scanning the room. She spotted a set of maroon chairs, a television, and two unopened windows.

Where was her counterpart?

"Mom, Dad, wh-what happened? Where's Sam?"

"Sweetie . . ." Her mother looked at the floor. "You were in a car accident. Sam didn't make it, honey. He died in the crash."

"It's his fault you're even in here," Johnny said bitterly, staring out the window and shaking his head. "The boy was reckless."

"Johnny!" Mona glared at her husband.

It wasn't a dream then, Lynaly thought, closing her eyes momentarily. She felt nothing. Only numbness. "How long have I been unconscious?"

"About two weeks," Johnny said. He appeared to be fighting to keep his voice steady. "The doctors weren't sure you'd ever wake up, though. It's incredible you're awake, even now."

"I can't believe that . . . he's gone."

Mona nodded. Tears streamed down her face. "Peter and Mary-Ellen held a wonderful service for Samael, honey. They wished you could have been there and passed along their hopes that you'd recover."

No feelings came to Lynaly, and none departed. She didn't cry or weep—it felt like some of the emptiness from when she met Lilly had followed her. Looking out the window to her left, beyond the IV drip and various monitors that beeped and bleeped, all she could think about was the vision and what Lilly had foretold, what she had offered.

I'll get better, and I'll go to Kerouac's. That book will be mine.

Then, a voice joined her thoughts. A familiar voice.

"*I am still with you, dear,*" said Lilly, "*as is Samael. You will get better, your strength will return, and you will begin your adventure by obtaining my hymn.*"

Sam piped in.

"*Lynaly, what I have left, I give to you. You will see in time.*"

She felt sadness well up within. *Sam . . .*

The voices fell silent, and a soft knock was on the door. A man with a bushy handlebar mustache entered. The sun reflected off his bald head. He wore a white lab coat over blue scrubs, and a black stethoscope hung around his neck.

"Hello, Lynaly!" the doctor said, eyeing her as he approached. "It's fantastic to see you awake. I trust you're comfortable?"

She gave a slight nod in reply.

"Excellent! My name is Doctor Anthony Betty. I'm your lead doctor. Doctors Malstrem and Yorkivich are your surgeon and neurologist. They're both with other patients, so I'll bring you up to speed.

"As you're likely aware, you were in a motor vehicle accident. You suffered a traumatic brain injury, as well as several subdural hematomas, or bleeds, on your brain. You also broke several ribs, your left leg, and your left arm. Both your lungs collapsed, and a few other vital organs were dealt a serious blow. There was massive internal bleeding. Really?"—Doctor Betty paused and looked at her parents—"you shouldn't be alive. Your survival is truly a miracle."

Johnny smiled and placed his hands on his hips. "Well, she's stubborn like her old man."

Mona rolled her eyes, but Doctor Betty chuckled.

"Indeed, indeed, well then." He looked back at Lynaly and clasped his hands. "We'll need to run a few tests on you today." As he removed the stethoscope from around his neck, Lynaly was struck by how much it resembled a noose. "We have you scheduled for a CAT scan and an MRI."

"In other words," her father said, smiling down at her, "you're going to be glowing in no time."

Lynaly cracked a half-smile. *Always the joker*, she thought.

After listening to his patient's heart and lungs, Doctor Betty tested her extremities, took her chart, and removed a pen from his coat pocket. "Do you feel any pain in your arms or legs?"

Lynaly shook her head.

"Any pain in your abdominal region?"

Again, she shook her head.

He frowned. "That's quite interesting. Well then, we'll run an EMG to check the nerves."

Johnny winced. "Is there something the matter, Doctor?"

The doctor rubbed his head. "Well, her heart seems fine. So do her lungs. But I don't understand why she's not sensing any pain."

"Perhaps she has a high pain tolerance?" Mona said.

"No, there should be a noticeable sensation with these breaks." He stood. "We'll see when we run the other tests and go from there." Doctor Betty then excused himself and left the room.

"You'll be OK, sweetie," Mona said, brushing golden locks of hair away from her daughter's face.

Johnny checked his watch. "It's about three, Mona—do you want to get something to eat? We still have some paperwork from school to do as well. Give Lynaly a moment to collect herself before they poke and prod her like some lab monkey?"

Mona nodded and kissed Lynaly's forehead. "We'll be back in a while, sweetie."

Lynaly smiled faintly at her parents. Her dad gave a little wave and closed the door behind them.

Suddenly, she was aware of how uncomfortable the bed was and how monotonous the machines' dull beeping and bleeping were.

"I've got to get out of this place," she muttered, gazing at the windows and the bright world outside.

And then, finally, her mind settled on the image of Sam, lifeless. Tears rolled down her cheeks.

Sam . . .

)

Lynaly drifted in and out of consciousness until she felt the bed shifting and jerking beneath her.

"Wh-what's going on?" Lynaly pulled the paper-thin sheets up to her chin.

Dr. Betty appeared amidst several oppressors, all hiding behind medical masks. "We're going to have you go through a few scans. Are you claustrophobic?"

She hesitated, unable to remember if she minded being confined in tight places. "I . . . I don't think so."

Dr. Betty nodded, and then the bed was in motion, monitors and IV drip traveling alongside.

After a quick trip through the halls, Lynaly was lifted onto the CAT scan machine's "bed" and instructed to take several deep breaths and breathe normally. The machine hummed loudly. Lynaly noted the distinct smell of the contrast dye injected into her veins. After the test was complete, the procedure was repeated in the MRI machine.

"Now, this will be very loud," the doctor said. "If you want to end the testing, press this button, and we'll remove you, OK?" He placed a device in her hand, and she nodded.

And then, she was alone again. In the belly of the beast, Lynaly felt the air still. Time seemed to stop. The monster shifted her around in its mouth as though chewing her up. She suddenly felt cold. Darkness poured into the already blackened space, burying her alive. She didn't panic but instead welcomed its presence. Closing her eyes, she let the sense of relief wash over her.

)

Lilith considered how best to move things forward in the deep corners of her soon-to-be vessel's mind. *I need to come into control of the body—that boy's soul fragment is the only thing keeping me here now. It's not his fault he had a soul fragment in his possession, the poor fool.*

She smirked. *How easy it was to persuade him.* Then she sighed. *But I need the rest to complete the ritual. I am sure the other exists in this period as well. Yes, yes, I can sense him—that bastard. He's occupying a vessel. I almost believed the boy was his incarnation.*

Anger stirred in the darkness for a moment.

Oh well, mistakes are made—trial and error, after all. I will acquire the rest and gain the power I deserve. I do not need to resurrect . . . him . . . anymore. Humans are so easy to string along, especially when it comes to love. Though I suppose I, too, was a fool.

However, times change. *Stay the course, Lilith.*

I'll crush the remnants of that hypocrite and then that betrayer of a brother and his little band of merry misfits.

Lilith smiled. Yes, *things will be different.*

)

An eternity or perhaps only moments later, Lynaly awoke to find herself back in her hospital room. On her wrists were restraints that bound her to her bed.

She struggled to free herself, groaning and causing a commotion. "Why can't I move!"

The cue-ball-headed doctor appeared. "Ah, I see you're awake! Good, good." He half-smiled but kept his distance.

"Why am I strapped to my bed?" Lynaly said, glaring at him and continuing to thrash about. "What the hell are you people doing!"

"You had quite a violent episode, miss. You nearly took the head off one of the attendants when we tried to pull you out of the MRI machine. This is for our protection as well as yours."

"Violent episode?" Lynaly said, her anger giving way to bewilderment. She lay back down. "I only remember falling asleep."

"Your reaction may be associated with post-traumatic stress disorder, a result of the accident," he said, stroking his mustache.

"I'd love to rip that mustache off your face."

The words popped into her mind, startling her. The thought hadn't been hers.

She cleared her throat. "So, what did the scans show? Anything?"

"Well, right now, you're showing no signs of breaks, and most of your other injuries have healed as well. Either you're an alien or a living example of God's gifts!" He grinned and continued stroking his stupid mustache.

Lynaly sensed anger rising again but suppressed it. "So, will I be able to get out soon then?"

The doctor paused and folded his arms across his chest. "I can't believe I'm saying this, but I don't see why not. You're in fine shape, and everything seems to be in order. We'll talk about it when your parents return. Until then, I suggest you get some sleep, Ms. Sargent."

As the doctor left the room, the thought *About time* crossed her mind. She cracked a smile and almost burst into laughter. Unsure where the odd emotions were coming from, Lynaly shrugged it off as a side effect of the pain medication. It was the only plausible explanation.

CHAPTER 2

HOURS PASSED. OUTSIDE LYNALY'S window, the streets of Ingram bustled. Horns blared their rage while people shouted at each other.

Lynaly's parents returned, the cue-ball-headed doctor following closely behind, flashing his stupid grin under the horrible mustache.

"Ah, you're awake, Lynaly. Excellent," Doctor Betty said. "I've just told your parents the good news, but we all agree it's a good idea for you to stay one more night—just for observation."

"We're so happy you're going to be coming home, sweetie," Mona said, wiping away tears.

"I'm sure you're gonna be glad to get out of here, kiddo," Johnny said. "We'll get you some real food and into your bed."

Lynaly gave a half-smile in reply. All she could think about was finally visiting Kerouac's shop.

After her parents left for the night, she drifted into a dream: There was a tall, thin man with a stubble-covered face. And there was also a sign whose words were blurred. All she could make out was "ton" at the end of a word.

In the witching hour, a familiar woman spoke to her. "He will return. He will awaken. Hurry, for time runs out, and with it, the chance to revive him."

Lynaly tossed and turned, the image of Sam's phantom lingering by her bedside. With a sigh, she whispered the words they often spoke to each other: "I'm yours, you're mine."

)

The sun wrapped its warming arms around the slumbering girl and ran its golden fingers through her hair, panning over the elegant curves of her cheeks, gently waking her. The chirping of birds and the humming of insects contrasted the hustle and bustle of Ingram's daily commuters. Iron beasts rumbled through the streets, rushing to their destinations.

Lynaly rose from her reclined position and placed her bare feet upon the icy tiles. A shiver writhed its way up her legs as she moved to the window, her white hospital gown crinkling.

A smile sprawled across her face. *Today, I finally say goodbye to this place. I can finally work on getting Sam back.*

Her reflection stared back and almost seemed to wave goodbye of its own accord. Hearing the door slowly open, Lynaly turned around to face the intruder.

"Oh, hey, kiddo," her dad said. Mona was behind him. "Didn't know you were getting up this early. Had I known, I would have told your mother to bring you breakfast."

"Oh, don't even start, Johnny," Mona said. "You were the one who just *had* to have breakfast before we left." She sighed and looked at Lynaly. "Really, sweetie, I just wanted to come get you out of here and take you home."

Lynaly smiled. "It's OK, Mom, I don't mind. I know you're both busy."

"That's my girl, always thinking of others," Johnny said.

"Well then, what say we get you ready and jet out of here?" Mona held up a small black bag and placed it on the bed. "There's a change of clothes in here. We'll leave you alone so you can get dressed, sweetie. Let us know if you need any help, OK?"

Once her parents had left, Lynaly pulled a black skirt and white blouse out of the bag, along with some underwear and a pair of red-and-black-striped calf-length stockings—her favorite. After dressing, she tossed the backpack on and headed to the bathroom, where she gazed upon herself. The blouse and skirt emphasized her hourglass shape.

"*Hmm . . . Not bad, my dear. You'll be able to use your beauty to your advantage when needed later.*"

"*I'll remember that, Lilly. Thank you.*"

She headed for the door. In the hall, her parents conversed with Dr. Betty, who waved at the awakened beauty.

"Good to see you up. I've scheduled several follow-up appointments, so I'll see you again soon. In the meantime, I wish you the best of luck. It was a pleasure meeting you." He shook her hand and then her parents' hands before disappearing down the busy hallway.

Johnny pulled a wheelchair over for Lynaly. Taking in her puzzled stare, he frowned. "Well, if you're certain you can walk on your own two feet . . ."

Lynaly rolled her eyes. "I'm pretty sure I can, seeing as how I was standing—and still am."

"Heh, fair enough, I suppose." Johnny set the wheelchair aside.

The hallways resembled clogged arteries. As she and her parents waded through them and into the packed elevators, Lynaly grew increasingly impatient. *What will it take to get to Kerouac's?*

When the elevator doors opened on the ground floor, Lynaly walked out quickly, ahead of her parents. She took a deep breath of the fresh air in the valet loop. Her nostrils flared as cool April air rushed into her lungs, filling her with a sense of freedom. At long last, she was out. Johnny and Mona came up behind her, each placing a hand on her shoulders.

"Well, sweetie, how does it feel to be back out in the world?" Mona smiled. "Bet you can't wait to get home—someone's been missing you for quite some time." She patted Lynaly's back.

Sheila, Lynaly thought, smiling.

"Yeah, I missed home," Lynaly said as her father led them to the family's sedan, noting the gaudy school staff sticker. Her mother opened the rear passenger door for her, and Lynaly buckled herself in.

As Johnny steered the car toward their quiet home, far from Kerouac's, far from where Sam had died, Lynaly tried to formulate a plan. *What do I do now? I won't be able to convince them to let me go to Kerouac's alone.*

Lilly's voice piped up. *"Ask them to take you right now. Play the sympathy card, and shed some tears. They'll give in and abide by your demands."*

She supposed it could work.

She raised her head and leaned toward the front of the car. "Mom, Dad, can you take me to Kerouac's Relics and Antiquities, please?" she said, a slight tremble in her voice. "It's very important to me."

Silence fell upon the car's interior. Her parents exchanged glances, and then her mother sighed heavily. Johnny nodded.

"I suppose we could," Mona said, concern underlying her tone. "Just . . . are you sure, honey? I mean, I don't want you to stress yourself out."

"Yes, Mom, I'll be fine. I want to visit it for some closure since that's where Sam and I were going." She met the gaze of her reflection, who flashed a hint of a smile.

)

Kerouac's Relics and Antiquities was housed in an ominous, lone, weathered brick building on the corner of an intersection. Two giant oak trees stood guard on either side of the entrance. The arched doorway was ten feet high, and the doors were solid oak carved with flowers and figures. Roman numerals from one to one hundred were carved into the arch. Various Latin scriptures were scribed on stained glass with images, and the shop's few windows were lined.

As Lynaly opened the heavy doors, musty, stale air wafted out. Stepping inside, she found herself in a world of wonder.

The walls were stacked top to bottom with tomes and texts. Ladders stood at the ready. A balcony protruded from the second floor, where more books could be seen, and old-fashioned weaponry hung upon the only wall not covered in books.

A tall figure carved out of wood graced the front of the shop. Her form was slender, her breasts bare, and a tail wound up her legs and torso. Bangles shackled her wrists. One hand lay upon her stomach while the other reached toward the sky. A leaf headpiece adorned her forehead, and long, flowing hair poured down the sides of her face, shrouding her in mystery. There was something familiar about the figure, but Lynaly couldn't put her finger on it.

The gray wood floors creaked with each step as she moved further into the shop, gazing in awe at the spectacle around her. She noted relics, such as crosses of gold and silver and other ornate fixtures in glass cases and scrolls encased in a wooden tower.

She made her way to the back of the shop, where an island of glass cases sat obedient, waiting. Atop one of the cases was a rickety cash register. Behind it, a black-leather barstool stood in a depression. Above a doorway that led further back was a small sign that read, "Employees only, please." Beside the doorway, miscellaneous boxes were stacked up to the ceiling.

She shifted her gaze to the gems, pendants, and other obscurities in the glass cases. Then, her eye was drawn to a rather large book on top of one of the enclosures. Across the cover of the worn and weathered leather-bound tome were foreign words scripted with elegant precision.

Lynaly opened the book and squinted at the text's preface. "Is this a collection of songs?" she asked herself.

A raspy, winded voice came from the room behind the counter as she turned the page. "Yes, it is indeed a collection of songs, young lady."

A hunched older man emerged. His long, silvered hair was pulled back into a thin ponytail. His eyes were white, glazed over from the erasure of sight. He walked with a black wooden cane containing various scripts and embellishments. Heavily wrinkled skin seemed to hang off his frail bones, yet his spirit seemed young.

He stopped behind the glass case in front of Lynaly and beamed. "Ah, you are the girl that boy told me about. Such a tragedy, indeed, indeed." The older man shook his head, sighing. "Tell me, young lady, does your mind often wander upon thoughts of Samael?"

Lynaly stood bewildered. How could he know so much about her? And how could he know who she was, given that he'd been robbed of his sight?

Seemingly noting her confusion, he continued. "Come now, child, I may be old and have no sight, but you learn to develop other methods of seeing the world and those in its clutches."

She still couldn't grasp it. "How do you know where everything is in the shop?"

"Well, each book has a unique scent. For example,"—he picked up the book in front of Lynaly—"this one smells like a sweet rose." He paused and then chuckled. "Plus, I have an assistant."

A silence fell before Lynaly replied to his question. "Yes, I dream of him often. I can still see him whenever I close my eyes as I did on our last day together."

"Ah, your words ring of truth. Sam had such promise. And he praised you daily, that boy. You must serve his memory well." The man crouched behind the counter, and when he straightened, he held a small black box. Setting it on the counter, he pushed it toward her, smiling. "Open it, young lady. I believe he would want you to have them."

Intrigued, Lynaly removed the top of the box to reveal a pair of inverted cross earrings, each with a garnet teardrop at the tip. There was also a choker adorned with the same inverted cross, a garnet teardrop at its tip.

"They're beautiful," she said with a smile. Then she returned her gaze to the older man, who smiled radiantly.

"Try them on later," he said, motioning toward the entrance. "Your parents are getting restless."

Lynaly smiled at the wizened man. "I also need the book. How much will that be?"

"Everything has been arranged. Sam took care of it."

"Thank you, sir," Lynaly said, pleasantly surprised.

"Call me Kero, young lady. I bid you farewell."

Back in her parents' car, Lynaly opened the small black box again and felt a strange sensation overcome her as if her consciousness were being subverted.

She thought about the unusual, spectacular items, examining the earrings and choker. *Sam, thank you.*

After closing the box, she ran her fingers along the spine of the old book, whose pages had yellowed. A golden clasp bound the tome shut. The leather did indeed give off a faint smell of roses.

"*Read this text tonight, young Lynaly,*" Lilly said.

And then came Sam's voice. "*You will not regret it.*"

She looked up at the window. The sun beamed upon her face, and a smile slowly drew from ear to ear.

)

It wasn't long before the white house and picket fence appeared. On the front porch sat a black puffball, waiting. Lynaly dashed out of the car and scooped up the black majesty, who joyfully meowed.

"Oh, Sheila! Did you miss me, sweetie? Yes, you did, oh yes, you did." Lynaly smiled as the black cat began to purr.

Sheila opened her big golden eyes to gaze at Lynaly, letting another meow escape. "C'mon, baby girl, let's go inside."

Lynaly trotted into the house and up the oak stairs, clutching the cat, box, and book tightly. She made an abrupt left turn at the top of the stairs, bringing her to the enclosure that offered solace. Sheila sprung from her arms onto the bed that had sat untouched for two weeks. After circling the middle of the twin bed, she plopped down, her tail wrapped tightly around her body, purring and waiting for Lynaly.

Lynaly placed the book and the box on the foot of the bed and closed the door behind her. She took a moment to admire her room, so happy to be back. The ample space contained a long cherry-wood dresser with a matching vanity mirror that spanned its length and a cherry-red parlor chair holding several stuffed animals. Beside the bed was a matching cherry-wood nightstand, part of a set her parents had bought for her long ago. On the opposite side of the room was the walk-in closet.

She removed her sneakers and settled herself on the bed beside Sheila. Picking up the small black box, she removed its top again.

Such fabulous earrings. The choker isn't my usual style, but that's okay.

She placed the choker around her neck and then wore matching earrings. Again, she felt the strange sensation but discarded it.

It's just the jitters.

For now, excitement was at the wheel. If correct, this tome would be a stepping-stone to getting Sam back. From where she sat, she could see the red gems sparkling in her reflection in the mirror.

She reached forward and slid her hands over the book's cover and spine. There was a *click* as she undid the clasp. The book opened, revealing several hundred pages in a language unknown to her. Her eyes wandered from images to text. Sheila stretched and sat up, meowing at her queen.

"There, there, Sheila," she said, glancing at her cat. "It's quite all right. We're going to find a way to bring Sam back! Isn't that wonderful?"

Lynaly smiled at Sheila, who seemed to smile in reply with a happy meow. Turning back to the book, she noted images of inverted crosses similar to those in her possession.

Hmm . . .

Lynaly became more and more fascinated by the tome's contents. Some translations had been written on sticky notes. *Resurrection* was scribbled on one tab, and under it lay the original text followed by the translation:

Audi me. Lilitu audite vocem meam. Quacumque die invocavero te, ut hereditate tua potentia et sapientia.

"Hear me," Lynaly muttered. "Lilith, hear my voice. I call upon you to inherit your power and wisdom."

Just then, Sheila shrieked and jumped to the floor.

Lynaly was startled with surprise and drew back from the book. "What the hell was that all about?" Her heart raced as she slowly looked back at the tome. Its once foreign text was now clear as day. Her eyes widened.

Lilly spoke softly in her mind. "*Please, allow me.*" The pages fluttered and stopped upon a hymn. "*Sing this in my name, and the deal shall be sealed. Your love will return, my dear.*"

Lynaly curled up her lips excitedly and began studying the hymn's directions. It called for a large number of volunteers. It also required that whoever wished to channel the spell be willing to offer themselves as a vessel.

Of course, Lynaly thought. *I would give anything.*

She rubbed her head, a migraine coming on strong. "I think I'll lie down awhile," she said aloud.

A feeling of unease came over Lynaly, So she closed the book and disposed of it on her nightstand. Sliding herself under the warmth of her blankets, she allowed them to caress her body.

Sheila jumped back on the bed and curled beside Lynaly's chest, purring. When Lynaly's parents poked their heads into the room to check on their daughter, she was sound asleep.

)

Night came, creeping from the mist of the unknown. The sky was pitch black, and the air was heavy. Sheila had turned onto her back, her tiny legs sprawled. Lynaly remained untouched, unmoved by the night, hunger, and any disturbance.

The house was silent except for the sound of the inhabitants' breath.

But outside, a shadow crept.

After seeping into the foundation's cracks, it rushed in a flurry of rage to the top of the basement stairs before floating across the light oak floor to a second set of stairs. It leaped to the top in a single bound and idled.

Suddenly alert, Sheila flipped over and nuzzled Lynaly. But her queen remained asleep.

And then the silence was broken.

Lynaly's bedroom door burst open, and a pale shade hissed at the feline standing guard. A ghostly voice echoed from the shade. "Begone, beast, for my quarrel is not with you. Stay you by her side, and I shall have to abide!"

This time, Sheila hissed, swiping in the shade's direction.

"Your actions, though heroic, are in vain. Can you not see the girl is possessed by the immortally insane? She must be wrested of her life, for she will slay all with her invisible knife!" The silhouette drew nearer, readying his blade.

"You will not harm her, you pathetic wretch!" a voice boomed. "It is far too late for you to intervene. She has already called *me* forth."

The shade startled and took several steps back. "No! It cannot be. How can it be that you were set free?"

The voice cackled, bringing Lynaly to sit up in bed. "For my first act in my new mortal shell, I will feast upon your blood and soul!"

Lynaly sprang from the bed and darted at the shade, who swung his blade at her. Instinctively, she grew her fingernails to a lethal length, threw the ghostly figure against the wall, and scratched out his eyes. "You aided in banishing me long ago, you pathetic fool. Now, I will make sure you go where you belong."

Warm bursts of liquid splashed her skin as she clawed wildly at the shade's chest, marking her pale complexion cherry red in the night. The shade wriggled free and rolled along the carpet to the window.

"You will be nothing without the book, foul demon," cried the shade. "You will be banished to the darkest depths of Hell!" Against the moon's light, the shade seemed to have its aura.

"Your tricks and tactics will not save you, you piss-poor excuse of a herald of the light. Your end"—Lynaly suddenly appeared before the shade, whose eyes were wide and horrified— "is now."

In a swift motion, she ripped the heart out of the shade. Blood poured over Lynaly's hands as the shadow collapsed to the ground, lifeless. Her fingernails retracted to normalcy.

Footsteps trampled into the room, and the light flicked on, revealing a blood-soaked Lynaly. Blotches of red splattered the walls, and a pool of crimson expanded under the lifeless body of a man dressed in black leather. A steel knife lay next to him.

Horrified, Lynaly's parents stood in shock in their matching blue PJs. Then Mona rushed to her bloodied daughter. "Oh my God, Lynaly, are you OK, sweetie?"

Lynaly bent down, retrieved the shade's knife, and, in a fluid motion, slit Mona's throat clean open.

She then fixated on Johnny as he stepped back, his eyes wide. "Lynaly, what are you doing? What have you done?"

Before Johnny had time to react further, Lynaly thrust the dagger into the depths of his abdomen. The red of his blood contrasted with the blue of his PJs. As he dropped to his knees, Lynaly twisted the dagger and brought the blade up, ripping open his rib cage and stopping at his sternum.

"You would have only gotten in the way, Johnny," Lynaly said calmly as the man faded away. "Your daughter is better off with no ties. I suppose, as a courtesy, you both can retain your souls."

Tossing the knife back to the floor and looking around the room, Lynaly curled her lip and sighed. "What a mess to deal with."

She moved briskly to the walk-in closet and gazed upon the various black and white blouses and skirts. There were also shelves full of blue jeans and outdated clothes. "Oh no, dear, this simply will not do."

Feeling blood trickle down her fingers, she brought her hand up and sucked them clean. "Yes," she said with a smile, "I believe it's time for a change."

She caught her reflection in the mirror. "Don't worry, my dear, I'll take care of things here. It'll be an award-winning performance."

)

Lynaly collapsed to the bed. Gathering her knees to her chest, she rocked back and forth. She was aware of the banshee wail of sirens approaching, and then red and blue lights bounced off the walls in a seizure-inducing schematic.

Footsteps marched up the stairs, and a blue blob appeared in her peripheral vision.

"Miss, are you all right?" The blob spoke softly as it approached.

"H-he killed my parents, and I-I killed him," Lynaly said breathlessly, continuing to hug her knees tight to her chest and rock. "He was coming at me."

More blue blobs poured into the room.

"OK, miss, I must ask you to come with me. We need to investigate the room." The blob offered a hand. Lynaly ignored it and kept rocking.

The blob reached for his radio. "We need a medic in here. She's shaken up bad."

"Charlie and Ronny are on their way up," a static-filled voice replied. "Gus is coming up, too. He'll check her out."

"Copy that. Bennett out." The blob addressed her again. "Miss, a medic is coming to examine you."

Lynaly scanned the corpses of her parents and the unknown man in leather and remained silent.

"*How am I doing?*" asked Lilly. "*Pretty convincing, hmm?*"

"*Did they really have to die, though, Lilly?*" Lynaly asked.

"*My dear, you agreed to do whatever it took to get Sam back. Collateral damage can and does happen. Even if they were spared, your parents could have been taken hostage and killed by the same group that killed me . . . and your beloved Sam.*"

Lynaly was dumbstruck. "*What do you mean by the same group that killed Sam? You mean to say that they're responsible for the car accident?*"

"Yes," Lilly replied. "*They fear my power and what we could accomplish together. They do not want you to bring Sam back, nor do they approve of our little . . . arrangement now.*"

"OK," said Lynaly. "*Self-defense is one thing, but can we agree not to kill people mindlessly?*"

She sensed Lilly rolling her eyes.

"*Very well, my dear. However, know that I will not hesitate to protect you.*"

"*I appreciate your concern, Lilly.*"

An EMT entered, and two men were in tow. "Miss," he said gently, "I'm going to look you over."

Lynaly glanced up and met his green eyes. "I'm fine . . . I'm not hurt . . . I . . . I . . ." She broke down in a rage of tears, and the EMT put his hand on her shoulder.

"Miss, you're OK, but we must get you out of here. Detectives Stickler and Cromwell will escort you downstairs so they can ask you a few questions. OK?" The EMT held Lynaly's shoulder comfortingly.

She nodded and looked at the two men standing at her bedroom door. One was tall and thin, with graying hair and a beard. His hands were in the pockets of his long tan coat.

The other man was also tall but somewhat overweight. His short black hair was receding. He wore a black ensemble and munched on a candy bar while staring at Lynaly and the crime scene.

The detective with graying hair spoke first, approaching. "Ms. Sargent, my name is Detective Charles Stickler, and this is my partner, Ron Cromwell," he said, gesturing behind him. "It's unfortunate to meet you under these circumstances. We're very sorry for your loss. Please accept our condolences." He extended his hand, which Lynaly took. Detective Cromwell shifted the candy bar to his other hand and followed suit.

Stickler shot Cromwell a glare and whispered in his ear, "She's a victim, you ass, show some consideration!"

Cromwell rolled his eyes and grumbled incoherently, still chewing.

"I apologize," Stickler said, turning back to Lynaly. "My partner is . . . not very bright. But sacrifices must be made." He chuckled without humor.

Lynaly nodded slightly.

"*Oh, you have no idea . . .*" thought Lilly.

Stickler took it as a signal to continue. "Now, let's go downstairs to find out what happened."

As the detectives led her downstairs, Lynaly heard dresser drawers slamming and glanced back at her room. "They're not going to steal anything, are they?"

Stickler smiled. "No, no. I assure you they'll only take whatever is necessary for evidence, miss."

As they settled in the living room, Sheila appeared and curled beside Lynaly on the couch.

"That's a cute cat you got there," Stickler said. "Really fond of you, she is."

Cromwell took another bite and snorted. Pieces of caramel dripped from his lips. "Seems like a bad time to have a black cat."

"Detective Cromwell, if you'd please . . . refrain from your incredibly unneeded remarks?" Red-faced, Stickler turned away from his partner. "Forgive me, miss. He's not usually this outrageous."

"What? I'm just saying," Cromwell said, with a mouthful of candy bar. "Black cats are supposed to be a symbol of bad luck."

"It's quite all right. I'm aware of the common misconception about black cats." Lynaly couldn't stop a small smile from flashing across her face. *I might not have to put this act on for long if these fools keep this up.*

Cromwell snickered. "See? She knows, unlike Mr. Know Nothing here."

"You do like making my job difficult, don't you? Maybe I should drag you outside and give you a few reasons to throw you in one of those ambulances!"

"Ah, promises, promises, Charlie. All bark, no bite." Cromwell chewed the last of his candy bar, crumpled the wrapper, and placed it in his coat pocket.

Stickler sighed. "Again, I am terribly sorry, miss."

"Is this a common thing between you two? This act? Do you have some weird codependent relationship?" Lynaly cocked her head. "I just lost my parents and was viciously attacked while sleeping, and you arrive only to play games?"

The detectives eyed Lynaly and cleared their throats. "N-no, miss," Stickler said. "We just—"

"You seem to have a lot of personal issues that you bring with you on the job. Perhaps it'd be best if I requested the presence of a superior?"

The detectives exchanged a glance. "We apologize, miss," said Stickler. "Now, if we can get down to asking you a few questions."

Lynaly sat up poised, ready. "Ask what you need to."

"You say you were sleeping?" Cromwell said, pulling out a notepad from his coat pocket. "How did you hear the intruder?"

"Sheila woke me up with her hissing and cries," Lynaly said, gazing down at her cat.

"When did your parents enter your room?"

"When they heard me scream." She sniffled. "The man got off me and went after them." Then she started to sob. "After he killed my parents, he came after me, and . . . and I killed him!"

"Miss, do you know why this man came to your house?" Stickler asked gently. "Do you know him?"

"No, I've never seen him before in my life. I don't know why he was here. I . . . I was just sleeping. I'd just come home from the hospital earlier today. I was in a car accident."

"I see. I heard about this accident. . . and I'm sorry for your loss." Detective Stickler shook his head. "Such a tragedy."

"Do you have any other questions for me?" Lynaly asked through her streams of tears.

"Not at the moment, miss, but do you have any for us?"

She sniffled again. "How . . . how did he get in the house?"

"It seems he came in through the basement window, and, well, you know the rest." Stickler frowned with concern. "Now, is there anywhere you can stay? With friends? Family?"

"No. All my family is out of state, and I don't have close friends." Lynaly scooped up Sheila. "She's all I've got."

"I see. Well, I can't say I advise staying here. Gather what you need, and we'll arrange a room for you in the hotel on thirty-fourth and fifty-sixth, downtown Ingram." Stickler closed his notepad and tucked it in his pocket in unison with Cromwell.

Lynaly nodded. "I'll just need my book from my room if you don't mind. It's on the nightstand, next to my bed."

"Are you sure you don't need anything else?" Stickler asked. "Change of clothes, toiletries, etc.?"

"No. I'd rather not have anyone get my clothes or have to walk back to my room in its current state."

Cromwell eyed her warily, but Stickler nodded, reaching for his radio. "Hey, Bennett, can you get the book on the nightstand near the bed? Thanks."

A moment passed before a voice crackled through the radio. "We're tied up in here. Can you or Cromwell come up and get it?"

Cromwell rolled his eyes and glared at Stickler, who motioned his partner to get going.

The detective muttered "Dick" as he shuffled past Lynaly and Stickler.

"Fat fuck," Stickler quietly replied with a grin.

Detective Cromwell returned several moments later with Lynaly's book in hand. "What the hell is this about? Some voodoo?" He examined it for a moment.

"*Get your fat filthy paws off my tome, you insufferable worm! I should tear out your heart and devour it before your eyes.*"

"It's for my history class," Lynaly casually replied.

"Eh, one hell of a read you got here. Shame what they put you kids through these days. Well, here ya go." He handed it to Lynaly.

She smiled and thanked him. "Yes, it's incredible what we must endure. Gaining knowledge is such a task. It's not quite like stopping at the vending machine. Thank you, detectives. Good night." Lynaly scooped up her black fluff ball, which climbed onto Lynaly's shoulder, and stared back at Cromwell, an evil glint in her eyes.

)

"That is one creepy pussy, lemme tell ya," Cromwell said once the young woman and her cat were out of earshot.

"You stupid prick." Stickler slapped Cromwell upside the head. "How many times do I have to tell you—when we play the stupid pair, you must keep it tolerable. That's how we coax the nutjobs into giving up more information than they would otherwise. Let's hope that she doesn't go and file a report!"

Cromwell giggled. "Oh, baby. I love it when you slap me, Daddy."

Stickler shook his head in disbelief and moved toward the front door. "I swear, I get stuck with the short straw, and then some, every time." He watched Lynaly get into a white sedan.

"Don't ya think we should have driven her?" Cromwell said, walking up behind his partner. "I mean, what if she goes off the deep end and commits suicide?"

"As long as she doesn't file a bullshit report, who cares. Let's get this over with and get out of this hellhole." Stickler spat on the porch, then headed back upstairs, Cromwell in tow.

CHAPTER 3

THE NIGHT HAD FULLY descended upon the city. The hotel the police had provided was a bust—decrepit and infested. Lily was not going to let Lynaly stay in such conditions.

Under neon lights and on street corners, hustlers and prostitutes gathered. As strangers threw themselves at her parents' car, hoping for business, Lynaly couldn't help but frown with disgust.

The city was in her prime. She was a gluttonous, insatiable beast that consumed her children. The mating rituals occurred every night. Bare breasts and backsides lay upon graves, the dead unable to turn away. Adult shows, XXX booths, street-corner gambling—indeed, the night brought out the crazies.

All around were people whose eyes were red with ambition and whose pupils were the green of money. Shouts, cries, and moans pillaged every structure close to the curbside.

Traffic lights acted as beacons for the ravenous plague distillers, while lampposts stood vigilant, watching the night's promiscuous entities. The moon, almost full, high above the rot, was seemingly displeased with Ingram.

Lynaly looked up at the entity and could almost see it frowning at the acts committed under its gaze. As Lynaly glared, a cloud covered the spooked moon, freeing it from her wrath.

She recounted how the moon had had no problem with the heinous acts carried out when her brother betrayed her and was run through by the Order, nor with the innocent blood spilled by its members.

How times have changed, yet man hasn't.

Before long, she passed through downtown Ingram, where the day was Dr. Jekyll and the night was Mr. Hyde.

She parked her parents' car in the hotel's towering parking garage and then went to the lobby, carrying Sheila and her book.

Entering the vast, luxurious space, she was viewed by snobbish ladies and bigoted gentlemen who turned up their noses at the feline and the messy-looking girl.

A grand chandelier clung to the ceiling, sparkling like a billion diamonds. A red carpet surrounded the golden-brown tile, on which sat an exquisite fountain. Patrons had cast various coins into it, hoping to achieve their pathetic wishes.

Lynaly ran her eyes over the elegance. Light sconces adorned the walls; in their golden light, she felt as if she were situated inside an hourglass, trapped among the sands of time that flowed as people came and went instead of being surrounded by luxury. Couches, chairs, tables, and stools littered the space, some occupied by the finest hypocrites.

At the front desk, she was met by a man who appeared to be no older than nineteen. His brown hair was neatly combed. Clean-shaven, he had bushy eyebrows and bore an overpowering hint of cologne.

Head tilted slightly, Lynaly stared at him. "*He'd look like a clown if you were to mess the hair, beat the nose to a* *reddened pulp, and powder that pretty boy's face!"* *She smirked as the attendant greeted her warmly.

"Good evening, miss. My name is Wilbur. Will you be needing a room tonight?" He spoke with a relatively high voice.

Lynaly held back her laughter at the poor lad's expense. "Yes, I need a room. Perhaps for a week or longer."

Wilbur nodded. "Yes, miss, but so you know, pets cost an extra two-hundred-dollar non-refundable fee, plus a fifty-dollar cleaning fee."

Lynaly stared a hole through the young man, whose slightly open mouth didn't move as she spoke, nor did his gaze. "That's quite nice and all, but I just lost my parents . . . tonight," she said smoothly. "They were diced to pieces before my eyes, and I have already dealt with Ingram's two most idiotic detectives. Now, if you want my business, which you surely do, I believe you will make me a real offer. If you cannot, I will give you an offer to die for. Now, scurry along and gather your manager—or should I fire the place up ?"

Wilbur swallowed hard. "Y-yes, miss, excuse me." His voice cracked, bringing a smile to Lynaly's face. He trotted away like a lost fawn and returned with a gentleman in tails a moment later. His name tag read *Ted.* The man's bald, polished head reminded Lynaly of Buddha's belly. Perhaps she could rub it and ask for a vast fortune. The thought made her snicker.

"Good evening, Miss. Is there a problem?" The manager asked calmly, with a fake smile.

"Do not smooth talk me, *sir.* I wish to acquire a room for a week, possibly longer. Tonight, I witnessed my parents being killed just after I arrived home from the hospital. I was in hospital as a result of an accident in which I lost the love of my life. Now, having no friends or close family to stay with, I request a hotel room only to be told I must pay an outrageous fee so my only family member can stay with me. You, sir, will require no such thing from me. I will pay the normal rate."

She stroked Sheila gently. "She is fixed, well-trained, and responsible for my being alive. You have a hero in your midst, gentlemen; you should honor her. Or, if you'd like, I can make you an offer you'll spill your blood over. I recommend the first."

Lynaly fixed her eyes on the manager, and magenta flickered through them momentarily. "So, Ted? Do we have an arrangement?"

He appeared to be trying to assemble pieces of words into the shortest of sentences. "Ah, uh . . . ahem, excuse me. Very well. We ask only that your pet stays in the bathroom."

Lynaly smiled with joy at the power of her persuasion.

"Excellent, it shall be done. Now then, here is my information." She handed Wilbur a slip of paper containing her name, address, and credit card details. "If you have questions, ask me in the morning. Now then, please give me a key, and we'll be on our way." Lynaly extended her hand.

Wilbur looked at Ted in bewilderment. His manager gave a quick nod, reached under the counter, and handed Lynaly an ornate, old-fashioned key. "This is to a royal suite, Ms. Sargent. Please do enjoy your stay, and thank you. Don't hesitate to call the front desk with any concerns or questions."

Ted gave her another fake smile while Wilbur stared in awe.

"Thank you, I shall." Lynaly gave the pair a sadistic smile, glanced at the golden key, which bore 318 in its hilt, and walked toward the pair of stainless-steel elevators. She called an elevator, and the doors parted. Stepping in, she pressed the button bearing 3, which shone like a pure gold c oin.

"Oh, Sheila," she said, exhaustion setting in, "let's enjoy ourselves. You will, won't you?"

Sheila responded with a short meow and then purred.

Lynaly looked upon herself in the doors. Her reflection had an angelic beauty. The gold of her hair was amplified a hundredfold, and her pale skin was a perfect blend of butter and cream.

On the third floor, her reflection split to reveal a vast hallway. The few rooms on the floor were all royal suites. She shuffled her heavy feet along the golden-brown carpet and approached room 318 with relief. The key opened the dark oak door.

She placed Sheila on the ground, and they both stared into the awaited darkness. It had expected them for quite some time and invited them to "come in and stay awhile." The room wafted sweetness and desire. The oversized king bed's covers longed to envelop the weary girl and her furry feline.

Lynaly glanced down at Sheila, who stared back up at her queen. "Yes, my sweet, I believe we will make do."

Lynaly and Sheila entered the wholesome darkness, shutting the large oak door behind them. The moon's light attempted to seep through the crack between the heavy opaque curtains. Sheila wandered in, her tiny paws making indents in the soft carpet. Lynaly flipped the light switch to her left, and the room ignited in a soft amber glow, the dark shifting in favor of the light.

"However," Lynaly said jokingly, "you heard the man. You have to stay in the bathroom. You might have an accident." The black fluff ball stared back, unamused.

Lynaly scanned the room. Beside the lavish king bed was a nightstand occupied by a crystal lamp. An unremarkable alarm clock sat in front of it, facing the bed. Across from the bed was an ornate TV cabinet. At the back of the room were massive windows covered by thick curtains. Underneath the windows was an oak desk with a small white sign displaying "Free Wi-Fi." Adjacent to the desk was the bathroom.

She dropped her gaze to Sheila, who leaped onto the desk and squeezed her body through the part in the curtains to gaze at the city below.

"Has something caught your attention, my sweet?" Lynaly smiled as Sheila poked her head back through the curtains and meowed. Her golden eyes caught the moon's glow that soaked the streets below.

She then turned her attention to the girl within. "I want to be certain that you won't"—she hesitated—"regret having done what you did."

"I *won't*," Lynaly said from within. "*Whatever it takes.*"

She proceeded to remove the garnet earrings and choker. A return of senses resolved a sudden blank state as Lilly returned control of Lynaly's body to the young woman.

Lynaly patted herself. "I . . . I am me?"

"*I am still here, Lynaly*," said Lilly. "*As long as you are aware.*" Nodding, Lynaly placed the relic of a book atop the nightstand.

Sheila poked her head back through the curtains, meowing. Then she dashed toward the bed. Lynaly followed and settled herself on the comforter in a cross-legged position. Sheila moved into her lap, purring.

She sighed deeply. "Oh, Sheila, what will happen now?" Lynaly stared down at her cat, who opened her big golden eyes to meet her gaze.

"*How are you faring thus far, my child?*" asked Lilly.

"Fine, though I still can't believe what happened." Lynaly frowned sadly.

"*As we discussed, they would have only gotten in the way,*" Lilly said soothingly. "*It's better that it ended so, my dear.*"

"I know, but still . . . They were my parents. They really loved me and cared about me." Lynaly ran her fingers down Sheila's back with a sigh. "They didn't do anything to deserve their fate."

"*You would have been killed back there along with your parents if not for my quick decision. We may agree to disagree, but they were a piece on the board that would eventually lead you to your demise, my dear,*" Lilly said firmly.

Lynaly agreed, albeit reluctantly, cold logic trumping emotions.

Deciding she could use a bath, Lynaly headed to the bathroom. Sheila ran back to the windows, shrouding herself under the curtains. The cream bathtub had a high back and legs shaped like eagle claws clutching an orb—most promising. Lynaly removed her clothes as the tub filled and stood before the mirror. In the depths of her eyes, she saw Sam placing his hands upon her shoulders. Closing her eyes, she imagined his touch. Warm streams flowed down her cheeks, but she quickly wiped them away.

"Now isn't the time to fall victim to such emotions," she said to herself. "I have so much to do."

Over the noise of the water filling the tub, she heard Sheila growl. She poked her head out of the bathroom. "What's the matter, my darling?" The cat remained behind the curtains. Only her tail could be seen, lashing from side to side.

"She might sense a threat or someone trying to spy on us. Humans are curious creatures, after all," said Lilly.

Lynaly shrugged and then slipped into the warm water, allowing herself to relax. "I doubt anyone would try anything here. There are enough witnesses. And I can always use your abilities."

"Perhaps," Lilly said, "but your use of my abilities is extremely limited. It would be best to exercise caution, regardless."

"I suppose so. I'd have to put the jewelry on to use your power. That would be time spent dying." Lynaly then sighed. "This once, I will risk it."

After her soak, Lynaly wrapped herself in one of the room's white plush bathrobes and found Sheila still at the windows.

She turned the room's light off, bringing the darkness instantly. "Sheila, come here, my sweet."

The faithful cat dashed to the enormous bed and rested herself near Lynaly. She purred as Lynaly stroked her. "What say tomorrow we go shopping?" Lynaly smiled as Sheila meowed in agreement. "Then it's settled."

As Lynaly rested her head on the soft pillow, she listened to the voice echoing inside. The voice she knew so well.

"Lynaly, remember the hymn." Sam's voice broke for a moment. "If you sing of your love for me at the talent show, it will open the way for me to return. Lilly will help bring me back. I love you."

"I'm yours," Lynaly said aloud. "You're mine."

)

Her mind drifted to visions of a high school talent show. Lynaly sang of her love for Sam, and he slowly manifested in the material realm. She clung to him, and her vice-like grip bit into his being. Blood poured over her fingers, disgracing her pale person and pure-white dress. Seeing her crushed love, his body limp in her arms, she roared in agony as the school's inhabitants laughed.

Lynaly threw herself awake, tears falling, before dropping her head back onto the pillow. Her forehead was beaded with the sweat of a thrashing slumber. Rolling to her right side, she put her arm around a purring Sheila and was somewhat comforted.

"How I cannot wait for this to be over . . . To be one . . ." Lynaly sighed, her eyes resuming their heaviness.

)

Time flowed on, and its continuous streaming raged its wrath on the iridescent red of the alarm clock, which now read 9:02 a.m. The curtains had been slightly parted. Sheila sat at the windows again, her tail thrashing about as she growled at an unseen specter. Gold and blue poured through the glass, giving the room the feel of an aquarium.

The sun had reared its golden head. Its mane waved blissfully in the pastel blue that had soaked up the early morning's moon. Cold air twisted and contorted as it meandered between the city's buildings. Dr. Jekyll was stretching his limbs. Ingram had reverted to its prim and proper self. Lynaly rolled over, her tired eyes aching in the light, a stranger that had found its way into her room.

Gazing upon the clock, she let a growl of her escape, unhappy that time was greeting her with such laughter. She threw her legs over the side of the bed and readjusted the bathrobe she'd fallen asleep in.

A small black box atop the desk immediately caught her eye. It hadn't been there when she fell asleep. Sheila meowed, greeting her queen as she moved toward the desk. Lynaly smiled and rubbed Sheila behind her ears while picking up the box with no tag.

Where could this have come from? Inside, she felt a smile linger.

As Lynaly sat down on the edge of the bed, Sheila scampered into her lap. She opened the box to find a white-gold ring with a marquise-cut garnet in its center. She gazed at its splendor, intricate design, and small hands holding the garnet. The band was designed to wrap around a finger like a tail, its tip curling near the stone. On the inside of the band were small words in a once-foreign tongue: *Protection, Strength, Wisdom, Longevity.* Between the words were small icons depicting the elements.

As she stared at the ring, a sense of familiarity overcame her.

A smile completed itself on her face. *Sam . . . it was you, wasn't it?*

Sheila placed her paw on the ring, and Lynaly giggled. "Oh, OK, I was going to try it on, don't worry."

As Lynaly slipped the jewelry onto her ring finger, her eyes widened—an unseen force jolted its way into her being. Sheila closed her eyes, and her claws sank into Lynaly's leg before she jumped to the ground.

"Sheila!" Lynaly stared down at her precious, who now thrashed about.

"Sheila? Sheila! What's the matter? What's wrong?" Panic gripped Lynaly as she watched her companion groan and wince.

And then, just as suddenly as she'd started thrashing, Sheila sat up calmly and tucked her tail around herself, gazing up at her queen. A most familiar voice echoed in Lynaly's mind. "I'm sorry I drew your blood. Forgive me, Lynaly."

Lynaly stared at the cat, dumbfounded. "Sam? Are you . . . in Sheila?"

Sheila blinked. "Yes, my queen. I'm here. Now, I can at least stay by your side until I can return to my body."

Warm tears streamed down her cheeks as she picked up Sheila and nuzzled her. "Oh, Sam, I miss you so much."

"I know, but soon we can be together. We will be one." He gazed happily at her through Sheila's golden eyes.

She cleared her throat to regain her composure. "Will you accompany me today, Sam?"

Sheila blinked again. "Yes, of course."

Filled with energy, Lynaly gathered her clothes and proceeded to the bathroom. She stared into the mirror as she held up the choker and earrings.

"I trust you will accompany us as well?" Lynaly said.

Lilly spoke softly. "Of course, my child. I am here to protect you and to help reunite you."

Lynaly nodded and equipped herself with her sacred jewelry, one earring at a time, before locking the choker around her neck. A familiar rush flowed through Lynaly's body. The world spun, and her eyes opened to a new view.

"A day to stretch my legs again. I must thank you, my dear. Worry not—we shall outfit you finely." Lynaly smiled at herself in the mirror.

Returning to the bedroom, she noticed Sheila on the windowsill, staring out again. "Something caught your eye, my dear?"

"*Something isn't right. Be careful on your way out.*"

The room's phone rang, startling Sheila, and Lynaly scanned the space to locate the muffled annoyance. Pulling open the nightstand's top drawer, she was rewarded with an old, corded phone.

"Some attempt at hiding your cheapness," she muttered.

She picked up the receiver and was greeted by a series of grumbles. "I'm sorry, what did you say? Perhaps you'd like to repeat that more loudly?"

"Huh? Oh! Miss Sargent, my apologies. My partner here—"

"What do you wish to ask me, Detective Stickler?"

There was a pause.

"I'm calling to make sure you're safe. I hope you had a pleasant night?"

"Pleasant? Watching an intruder brutally slay my parents? Oh yes, Detective, I had a *very* pleasant night. Now, if you're done harassing me, I have matters to attend to. Unless, of course, you have something useful to say?"

Lynaly smiled as she listened to the silence. Then she heard someone mumbling over the sound of a crinkling snack wrapper. "Please tell Mr. Cromwell that I'm not speaking to him, only you, and to mind his tongue if he can bear it. I find talking to someone who chews with his mouth open rather insulting."

There was a snicker followed by what seemed to be a slap. "Okay, Miss Sargent. I trust you'll remain close if we have any further questions."

"Yes, Detective, I assure you I'll be in the area. Good day." She hung up and sighed. "Now then," she said, turning to Sheila, "that's over and done. Let's go, shall we?"

"*I'm coming.*" Sam's voice echoed in Lynaly's mind as Sheila ran to her.

She placed the book in the nightstand drawer, mumbling an incantation to ward off unsavory folk who might be interested in it, then closed the drawer before scooping up the black puffball with a smile.

As they made their way down the elevator, through the lobby, and then into the elevator for the garage, Lynaly couldn't shake the feeling that someone was watching them. Sheila, perched on her shoulder, peered through her hair and kept a lookout behind them.

"*Someone is following us.*"

"I am aware. They will show themselves when we get near. Do be ready, my sweet.

"*As you command, my queen.*" Sheila crept back, further hiding in the jungle of Lynaly's hair.

After the elevator had stopped on the third floor of the parking garage, Lynaly exited casually and strolled toward the white sedan.

The presence drew closer. A deep, raspy voice echoed through the garage. "You may fool these people, Lilly, but you cannot fool the all-seeing. Your plan will falter, and when it does, you will be cast back into the depths of Hell, where you belong. We will forge the shackles to bind you for eternity this time."

Lynaly stopped. "Why hide from my sight?" she said smoothly. "You speak of such acts, yet your tongue curls on the hypocrisy. You are all the same—annoyances, like bothersome flies that must be swatted. I will gladly be rid of you, pest."

Sheila jumped off her shoulder and crept stealthily into the shadows, stalking the specter.

"Surely you know me, Lilly."

A dark shadow crept out from behind a concrete pillar and then stretched itself into the shape of a human: a man with a pale complexion. His brown leather hood was pulled up. A crudely made wooden mask obscured the top half of his face, but a smile crawled along the bottom half. The white had been painted sloppily, and blood-red drips were streaked under the eyes. "What's the matter? Don't you recognize me?" He stepped under a light.

Lynaly frowned.

"Ah, is that any way to greet your brother?" He chuckled.

"Brother? You're sorely mistaken. No brother of mine would cower behind a flimsy clown mask." Lynaly tilted her head at the specter. "Besides, you look nothing like him, wraith."

This time, the man frowned. He took a few steps toward Lynaly, though his fluid movement could have been described as floating. Stopping under another light, the shade threw back his cowl, revealing his short, jagged white hair. He then removed the crude wooden mask.

His actual eyes were sewn shut with a thick black thread, but a red glow penetrated his eyelids. He was relatively young. A long scar ran from his right ear to the corner of his mouth—another hint of red under the light. His lips were gray with the absence of life, but his face was clean.

Tall and in top form, he had broad shoulders and sculpted arms. A black-leather harness stretched over his chest—the dyed deerskin vestment of a barbarian from ages long past. A massive black studded leather belt encompassed his waist. In the buckle was an infinity symbol inlaid with moonstones, garnets, and sapphires.

Tattoos covered every inch of his arms; various scriptures and chants wrapped their way around the beastly man. His forearms were covered in a series of bandages, withholding a secret. Through singed fingerless gloves, the white tips of his fingers glowed softly like light bulbs—but they would offer frostbite if directly touched. Black-leather pants disappeared into black boots laced up to his calves.

This was no mere grunt, and Lynaly knew it.

"I see the scar I gave you never healed," Lynaly said with a hiss. "I should have done worse, you traitorous bastard."

"All this time and not even a 'Hello, Atreyu'? You were never one for greetings, Lilly." The man's frown deepened.

"That was a name I let go of long ago, dear *brother*. Yet you dare flail it around, making a mockery of your ancestry. You are a hypocrite, and all for a deplorable 'god'? I sure hope your service doesn't involve suckling his teat. Or is it in the chance you may suck on something more?"

Seeing the anger show up on Atreyu's brow, Lynaly grinned.

"You mock me and the creator?" Atreyu snapped, baring his blue-gray teeth. Spit flung off his tongue.

"Ah, ah—shouldn't you put *him* before yourself? Again, such hypocrisy, dear *brother*." Lynaly's grin widened malevolently.

"I shall bring you back, my sister. I have been tasked with condemning you for your treacherous ways and your deplorable actions exacted upon the mortal of man." Atreyu clenched his right hand into a fist.

"Upon the mortal of man? Man is mortal—or have you forgotten? You were once a man and still are, Atreyu. Your seals keep your soul bound to your body but offer no immortality. You are a walking corpse, a shell of a shadow. A shallow husk of a man." Lynaly's voice rose to a shout. "You disgust me with your acts of 'righteousness'! You turned on your own family and offered us to the Crusaders, and for what? To keep your wretched body? Age has made you as pathetic and ignorant as man, Atreyu. I tire of your presence. Begone!" Lynaly swatted the air.

"No, dear sister," Atreyu said, treading toward her. "I will drag you back to the depths of Hell from whence you escaped. Only this time, you will be bound by the damned ice near the bane of the mighty traitor himself."

"I think not. I rather like being able to stretch my legs. And besides, I have a good thing going with this lovely girl. Would you harm an innocent to bring me to 'justice'? That would mean having a black mark on your record . . . my brother." Lynaly smiled as Atreyu halted. "That's right, you cannot harm an innocent, so as long as I'm here, you are, as they say here now, 'shit out of luck.'"

Atreyu gritted his teeth. "I don't care! If it damns me, so be it. I will be your jailor in Hell if need be."

Lynaly couldn't hide her surprise. This was not the brother she'd known.

Atreyu reached behind his back and retrieved two cross-shaped katars. In the middle of each was embedded a garnet, as red and as rich as the blood that could be freshly spilled.

"You wield the very same weapons you used to slay our parents and our little brother. How pleasant," Lynaly said with a snarl.

Atreyu placed his mask back over his face. Only his mouth was visible, and it widened in a smile. "Yes, the very same. I would have carved you with them had it not been for—"

"You will not mention *his* name to me! I have abandoned all feelings for that traitor, just as I have for you! So you want a fight? You've come to the right person!"

Lynaly readied herself with clenched fists and a hellish glare intent on incinerating the beast before her.

"Sheila! Come forth, my pet. From the shadows do stir. Let your prowess form into the stalker of the night!"

Lynaly's sacred jewelry glowed bright red, and a meow became a shrill roar. A monstrous panther leaped from the shadows at Atreyu.

"Ha!" Atreyu swung at the beast, who deflected the demon-hunter's attacks as if playing with its prey. "You must always rely on your pawns to do the work for you, weakling!"

"*I am no pawn, you foul excuse for a guardian!*" Sheila roared as she swatted at Atreyu, clawing his vestments and puncturing his skin.

"Gah! You fleabag! You miserable little lapdog, get out of my way!" Atreyu swung his blades, and a blunt edge knocked Sheila to the ground. He raised his katar high, ready to plunge it into the beast.

"No!" Lynaly dashed forward to protect her companion and used some magic to catch the blade with her hands. "I am tired of you, brother." She spat in Atreyu's face. "Never did I like having you around!"

"The feeling is mutual, dear sister!" Atreyu swung his other katar toward Lynaly. She backed away quickly, but his blade scratched her left arm.

Atreyu grinned as Lynaly bled. "Rusty in your possession, are you?"

"Actually, blood is just as useful when it runs." Lynaly grinned wickedly as she smeared some of the blood that had trickled down her arm into her hands. "I wonder if you remember this trick?"

Lynaly clapped her hands, and the garnets in her earrings, choker, and ring glowed a violent crimson. The inside of the garage began to spin. A heatwave slashed through the air and spiraled out in all directions as a bright magenta flame ignited in her palms. Boiling blood ran down her arm, feeding the fire.

"Perhaps you don't, seeing as how most of those who witnessed this are all dead as a result. Go, meet your maker!"

Lynaly expanded the flame in her hand and then hurled the enormous fireball at her brother. Time seemed to slow as Lynaly caught a glimpse of the words "Forgive me" on Atreyu's lips. She might have hesitated had she not believed it to be a distraction.

Flames spread over the man, and his flesh reddened before it slopped to the ground. His hair was consumed into nothingness, and his eyes flung open, released from their stitches, an unsettling blue-white beneath the red flame. Skin melted into the remnants of his clothes. His voice was muffled by the crackle of his flesh, sinew, and bone. His being was charred to a fine, pitch-black dust, and as the wind passed through the garage, it carried out his ashes and spread them over the city.

Lynaly sighed with relief, sunk to her knees, and turned to pet Sheila, who had reverted to her small, precious state. "You did good. I thank you for your actions, my pet."

Atreyu's voice reverberated through the parking garage. "I am far from gone, dear sister. One day, when you least expect it, I'll return. And when I do, I'll bind you to the depths of Hell."

Lynaly glanced around, waiting for a figure to appear. "I'll be waiting when you try but fail yet again, Atreyu."

When she was convinced Atreyu was gone, Lynaly climbed to her feet. "Come, Sheila," she said, scooping her up. "Let's continue what we set out to do."

"*Is what he says true, Lilly?*" Lynaly said in her mind. "*Did you commit those acts?*"

"I do what I must to survive. Atreyu betrayed my family and turned my most beloved treasure against me. As a result, I was confined to the Nether. When you free Sam, in turn, you will free me."

"*Whatever it takes. You've already helped us so much. Thank you.*"

Back in the white sedan, Lynaly glanced at her arm. The scratch had fully healed, leaving only a hint of a scar. The blood had seeped back into its life form, where it would continue to work.

)

As Lynaly cruised through Ingram's bustling streets, she peered into the rearview mirror and noted a police cruiser tailing her.

"It seems we'll have company on our outing," Lynaly said to a sleeping Sheila, curled up on the back seat. "No matter. The more, the merrier, I suppose." She grinned.

"*Do they suspect us?*" asked Lynaly as Lilly commanded her body.

"No, my dear, they will just follow, perhaps ask more useless questions. It's nothing to worry about."

This seemingly calmed the young woman within. "*Do whatever it takes to be rid of them—without killing them, please?*"

Lynaly smiled her agreement but was a tad disappointed. While she drove, she was aware of the congestion, the blaring horns, and the people hanging out their windows, cursing at one another. Some scuffled, and some even shot at each other.

She shook her head and sighed. "After all this time, nothing has changed. If anything, the methods of snuffing out a life have only improved."

The day was a more tamed beast than it once was, though. Or at least its wildness wasn't as noticeable.

Lynaly pulled into a public parking lot, and the police cruiser drifted by, its windows shaded. She rolled the windows down partially, leaving Sheila to sleep, exited the car, and walked to the small Gothic boutique shop just around the corner.

A breeze passed over her body, pulling back her long golden hair. The sun's cascading warmth upon her face perked her mood. She responded to the occasional glances of passersby, who noted the blotches of dried blood on her white blouse and black skirt with a devious smile, sending them off in a hurry.

"*My dear, it is time you distanced yourself from others. You are a special girl. Rather than blend in perfectly . . . yes. Yes, this shall work quite well.*"

Approaching the shop, Lynaly glanced at the sign, which replicated an old-fashioned theater marquee. The shop's name, The Slaughterhouse: Gothic, Horror & More, was displayed in black and red letters. Iron bars clung to the windows in a spiderweb fashion. She grasped the wrought-iron door handle, shaped like a skull and enveloped with vines and snakes, and pulled open the heavy oak door.

The walls were purple and full of clothing shelves. Ladders on tracks slid in circles around the store, and posters bearing classic horror scenes—cutthroats, werewolves, traditional vampires—witty quotes, bands, and artistic renderings adorned the tops of the high walls.

It was an above-average punk store for those who sought to define themselves further. Some fellow customers glanced at her bloodied get-up and gave her a nod and a smile, blissfully unaware of the truth.

A slow smile crept across Lynaly's face. It was the perfect place to find a suitable wardrobe—one in which she could be truer to herself.

A succession of guitar chords poured out of the speakers and found its way into the ears of those meandering about. A drumbeat and a clash of cymbals ushered in a glorious melody. A few words were offered. By this point, most would recognize the song: "The Killing Moon" by Echo & the Bunnymen. Amid the music, staff and customers conversed, decisions were made, and the door opened and closed, briefly allowing the corruption of the outside world to seep in before cutting it off again.

Lynaly spent her time wisely, obtaining belts, stockings, skirts, blouses, and bondage pants. At the register, she was greeted by a girl with long black hair. Her face was powdered white, and her bright green eyes were surrounded by heavy eyeliner. Her name tag read Annie.

"Excuse me," Lynaly said. "Do you have any dye? And where is your makeup selection?"

"Sure do!" Annie replied with energetic happiness. "It's right over here."

She escorted Lynaly to the makeup and hair dye center, tucked away from the clothing. Lynaly nodded. "I'll only be a moment."

"Take your time. There's no rush."

Lynaly feasted her eyes on the many different flavors, styles, and colors of makeup and dye.

Let's see. Something truer to . . . me. Since, after all, I will be in control.

Minutes later, she returned to the register. Annie greeted her enthusiastically once again. Her energy subtly annoyed Lynaly. "All set?"

"*She's way too chipper to be working in retail,*" Lynaly said from within, cringing.

"*What is this . . . retail?*"

"*I suppose it would be like Hell to you if you worked in it long enough.*"

Lynaly nodded. Annie rang up the order and pushed a button on the register. "Your total comes to three hundred and eighteen dollars and seventy-three cents. Are you interested in obtaining a store credit card? You would automatically be enrolled in our exclusive rewards program. You can also get fifteen percent off your purchase today."

"Are there always so many offers for such frivolous things? It's rather annoying," Lilly said.

"She means well. Be kind to her. I suppose the saying 'a little kindness goes a long way' would apply."

Lynaly forced a smile. "No, thanks." She swiped her card and signed.

"Here you are," Annie said, beaming and passing her the items she'd placed into bags. "Thanks! Enjoy your day, and come back again!"

Outside, Lynaly found Detectives Charles Stickler and Ronald Cromwell on either side of the door.

"Well, well, been doing some shopping, have we?" Detective Stickler grinned.

"With your parents' money, no doubt," Detective Cromwell chimed in with a stupid grin.

"Oh, I see," Lynaly snapped. "You two have nothing better to do than heckle a victim in mourning?"

"Well, Ms. Sargent," said Stickler, "it's hard to be convinced you're in mourning when you're here shopping. Especially if you put the items on your parents' account."

"Ah, so you think I was after my parents' money? Wrong, Tweedledee and Dumb. I used my card, which is attached to my account, which I pay for. So, your phishing adventure is further halted. Now, I'm sure you wouldn't want your superior to know you're harassing a victim." Lynaly smiled as the men grunted and mumbled under their breaths. "Good day, gentlemen."

Stickler dropped his gaze to the bloody blotches on her blouse. "Is that your blood or somebody else's?"

She looked down. "These? I accidentally cut myself. It's nothing to concern yourselves over. Again, good day, gentlemen."

Lynaly returned to the white sedan, where Sheila was awake and waiting. Her golden eyes peered out from the back seat of the car. "If you had asked, I would have ventured outside and waited to alarm you," Sheila yawned.

Lynaly stopped outside the rear door and smiled down at the black fuzzball. "It wasn't necessary, Sheila. Besides, you need your rest. Could you pop the trunk?"

Sheila cocked her head. "*Oh! Yes, I can.*" She hopped to the front and pushed the button.

After setting her bags in the trunk, Lynaly saw a figure on a nearby rooftop, eying her. When she angled herself to get a better look, the figure disappeared.

"Perhaps another glorified hunter? Or my dear brother? No matter. It's time for us to prepare to get Sam back. Isn't it, dear Lynaly?"

Lynaly smiled.

CHAPTER 4

IT HAD BEEN QUITE some time since Lynaly ate. The agonizing pains in her growling stomach reminded her of that. She winced slightly. She'd forgotten that she possessed a mortal, so she'd have to eat to nourish her host.

She sighed heavily as two quiet voices on the drive back to the hotel piped up nearly in unison.

"*Let's get some fast food!*" said Sheila.

"*Why not try a fast food place?*" said her host.

While she wasn't familiar with "fast food," she was intrigued by the thought. "Very well. What would you say is good?"

"*Sonic.*"

Lynaly glanced at the passenger seat, where Sheila drooled in anticipation.

"*Oh, yes, very satisfying. Oh, so tasty.*" The remnant of a soul harbored inside the furry body seemed to be enjoying memories of the place.

Lynaly smiled. "And so it shall be." She scanned the road. "Now to try to locate one."

She buzzed past a pair of golden-fried arches, a crowned king wildly grinning and holding a hamburger, and a red-haired girl in a country outfit. Before long, Lynaly pulled up to the drive-in area of the favored establishment, and Sheila practically leaped with joy. The scents of fresh

French fries, sizzling beef, and toasted buns wafted toward Lynaly, further angering her stomach. After looking over the menu, Lynaly placed her order. Sheila kneaded the passenger seat, waiting.

Minutes later, a young man—Lynaly guessed he was still in high school—rollerbladed toward her car carrying a vibrant red tray. His eyes met Lynaly's. "He-here's your order." He gazed bashfully at her.

"Thank you"—Lynaly smiled and glanced at his name tag—"Gerald."

He nodded shyly before returning to the hub. As Lynaly dug into the bag, Sheila stood on her hind legs, peering at its contents as they emerged one by one. Lynaly took a bite of a toasted bacon cheeseburger and was bombarded with many new flavors.

"Mmm, this is rather tasty," she said, taking another bite. "I used to live on meat and wine, but this is quite splendid."

Sheila stared on, her expression hopeful.

"I'm sorry, Sheila, I don't think you can have this."

The feline dropped her gaze, and then she turned in a circle on the passenger seat before lying down.

Her big golden eyes closed with disappointment. "It's *probably for the best. I wouldn't want to get too overweight or such.*"

"My dear," Lynaly said with a chuckle. "I only meant you couldn't have my burger. I have this for you." She removed the paper from another burger and placed it before Sheila. The fluff ball's disappointment faded as if it had never existed, and she set about devouring the magnificent slab of meat before her. Lynaly laughed, giving Sheila a pat on the head.

The cat purred while nibbling at the beast. "*Oh my, it's so good! Thank you, my queen!*"

When Lynaly's and Sheila's bellies were full and content, Lynaly continued the drive to the hotel. She fancied reading her book—well, getting the girl to read it so she'd be prepared for the upcoming talent show.

"*Lilly? Do you think I'll be able to memorize the words well enough?*"

"Yes, my dear, as what I know, you now know. On the day, you will speak the words. And then we shall set out on a new journey as one."

Back in the hotel's parking garage, Lynaly gathered her new clothes and accessories from the trunk, and then she and Sheila ventured back through the garage. She couldn't help but notice Atreyu's black scorch mark on the concrete floor. Lynaly felt a wave of sadness but instantly discarded the emotion—it was simply the mortal body giving in.

Exiting the elevator on her floor, she saw two figures standing by her door, their backs to her. Lynaly sighed loudly.

"Ah, Ms. Sargent," Detective Stickler said, turning around. "I see you've finally returned. We were getting worried."

As usual, Cromwell was munching on a king-sized candy bar. Lynaly wished he were eating the shit that came out of his mouth instead.

"Gonna be putting on a fashion show? Is your cat gonna watch?" Detective Cromwell took a bite.

Lynaly's face curled into an expression of disgust. "What brings you here besides further harassing me? Should I add 'stalking' to the list of charges?"

Stickler cleared his throat. "No, miss, we were merely checking to ensure you returned to the hotel safely. There were reports earlier of shouting in the parking garage. Unfortunately, surveillance could not pick anything up—just a bright red flash."

Lynaly stood there, expressionless, not offering anything for them to go on. "And? What does that have to do with me?"

"Well, it happened around the time you left this morning," Stickler said, adopting a cocky stance, his hands in his pockets. "We're just wondering if you saw or heard anything."

"Nope, now then, if you'll excuse me. I have to start a fashion show for my pussy . . . cat." Lynaly motioned the two detectives away from the door while Cromwell tried to stop himself from choking.

"I . . . can't breathe." He clung to his throat. Stickler socked him in the back, freeing the culprit, and Cromwell swallowed. "Mmm, peanut."

He turned just as Lynaly was about to close the door. "We could always help, just so you know."

Lynaly noticed his foolish grin speckled with chocolate and caramel. "I thought that peanut would be your undoing. What a pity."

She closed the door and peered through the peephole until the pair left her line of sight. "Disgusting," she said with a sigh. "Simply disgusting."

Sheila clambered onto the bed and rolled happily as Lynaly removed her new clothes from the many bags. She placed the hair dye and makeup in the bathroom. Then she gazed at her reflection in the bathroom mirror. "After tomorrow, my dear, you will never be quite the same."

Soft laughter came from within.

After meticulously hanging her outfit of choice for the approaching morrow on the bathroom door, Lynaly looked upon it. "Hmm, yes, this will do quite well."

Sheila tilted her head. "*Never thought you'd wear such an outfit.*"

"We aren't just anyone, my dear. Besides, I find this particular set rather intriguing."

Lynaly moved to the bed and removed her jewelry. She sat and scratched Sheila behind her ears, thinking of how tomorrow might pass.

So, I'll sing the words as instructed in the ritual. Overcome the trial as it presents itself. She wasn't sure how that would go or what precisely the complex wording meant, but she thought she had the gist. *If you're a strong magic user and complete the ritual, you gain the power invoked. And if you fail, you die.*

She sighed. It seemed complicated, but she knew ancient magics tended to be so. *At least I'll have Lilly's help.* Still, she couldn't help worrying about something that could put a wrench in everything.

The ritual needed willing volunteers.

I'm sure that the audience's presence will be enough. It's a shame that so many will die, but . . . I said that I'd get Sam back at any cost. I've already made a deal with Lilly and given up my parents, she thought sadly. *So what's the big deal if I offer up my classmates? It's not like any of them cared about me.*

Lynaly recalled the handful of students she regarded as friends but never really associated with outside school.

There was Shane. He was a decent guy.

Mostly, she'd spent her time with Sam. Images of the accident flooded her mind, and tears began to fall down her cheeks.

I need to stay the course and focus. Tomorrow . . . tomorrow will be the day I get Sam back!

)

Lynaly closed her eyes, retreating to the dark recesses of her mind. She and Lilly stood together in a moonlit realm, Lilly in front of her, preparing her for what was to come.

"Study the words," Lilly said. "They will come to your mind when you need them. May I remind you that after you perform the ritual, you will face a challenge—a safeguard designed to make you falter, instituted by those who would rather see you fail, my dear child. Hesitate, and it will be your end. And the end of Sam."

Lynaly looked up at Lilly, saddened.

"What is the matter, my dear?" Lilly tilted her head slightly.

"Will more people die because of me?"

Lilly paused. "Sacrifices must be made. If you withdraw from your intent, more will be lost. If you dare hesitate during the test, everything will end. I cannot help you with that."

"I know . . . I just want to be sure. I don't care what other people think, and as far as I'm concerned, I'm already dead. I died with Sam back in the car. But if I can help you, and if I can see him . . . be with him again." Lynaly shed a tear, which looked silver in the moonlight. "I said I'd do whatever it takes." Lynaly lifted her gaze to meet Lilly's.

"You are strong, Lynaly. You will see how beautiful everything will become." Lilly smiled as she placed a hand on Lynaly's face. "Weep not, for soon others will weep."

Lynaly grinned wickedly as Lilly opened her eyes for her. The hotel room looked the same; time had moved only slightly. "I cannot read the book for you. However, I will be able to help you retain the information. Perhaps a bath, then we can study."

At that, Lynaly removed her choker and earrings and bathed. She closed her eyes as she became familiar with her body again, letting the warm water soothe her.

It's strange not being in control—like I'm a pilot with nothing to maneuver. Just . . . a pair of eyes, not even a person who exists anymore. I wonder if that's how Lilly feels when I'm in full control.

After withdrawing from the tub, she wrapped herself in the luxurious plush robe provided by the hotel and removed the tome from the nightstand's drawer. Flipping through the musty pages, Lynaly gazed at the text. Then, quietly, she muttered the words of an ancient language.

)

Minutes became hours. The sun had long since deployed the darkness to replace it. Stars sparkled in the sea of black that wrapped itself around the city, whose streets were once again contaminated. Lynaly had memorized the verses and was able to recall them smoothly. She wandered to the windows. A thick cloud masked the moon, hiding it from her gaze.

On the ground, people ran rampant in packs. Whores stood on street corners, and dealers spread their filth. She frowned at the sight of the city—glorious by day, rabid, disease-infested by night.

"Perhaps one day I can clean the streets of these . . . pests," Lynaly muttered, her warm breath lightly steaming the window. Her reflection revealed she was grinning, no longer surprised by the thoughts of such acts.

After turning off the light, she climbed into the warm bed. Sheila shifted slightly to roll onto her back, her legs upwards.

"Will it all be worth it?"

"*My dear, once you see, you will truly know.*"

Sam . . . Lynaly sighed as dreamland approached to embrace the darkness.

)

During the night's endeavor, the telephone rang. Lynaly sprang up. "Who would be calling at this hour?"

She fumbled for the phone and picked up the receiver. "Hello?"

"Hello? Lynaly?"

She was surprised to hear the deep voice of her distant uncle. "Uncle Bartholomew?"

"I'm sorry to be calling you so late, kiddo, but I wanted to let you know that I'm handling your parents' affairs." He cleared his throat. "Look . . . I know you never saw me much or got the chance to get to know me. I want you to know that I will do everything possible to help make things easier for you now. After everything that's happened . . ." He let out a hacking cough to cover up his sob. "I'm sorry, Lynaly." He continued after clearing his throat again. "Your parents set up a trust fund for you, but you won't be able to access it until next year. I also figured you wouldn't want to stay in the same house where your parents were killed and all, so the vacation home in Middleton will be yours."

Lynaly raised her eyebrows. That would come in handy. "Thank you, Uncle Bartholomew."

He sniffled. "Now, if you need anything, don't hesitate to call me. I'll send all your things, plus some money, to Middleton."

She smiled. "Thanks again, Uncle Bartholomew. I appreciate it. Now, if you'll excuse me, I have to get some sleep for school."

"No problem, kiddo, take care."

As she hung up, Lynaly briefly recalled the spring and summer visits to Middleton. She remembered the town well and had enjoyed spending time there as a child.

Meanwhile, Lilly stewed in the depths of Lynaly's mind, reliving her memories of the quaint town.

"*Him. He's got to be there.*"

"Who, Lilly?" Piece by piece, Lynaly equipped herself with her jewelry to understand further.

The familiar rush of energy flowed through Lynaly's body.

She opened her eyes as she became Lilly again. "Someone who betrayed me long ago."

)

At last, the morning had come. The dark shroud of night was drawing back to reveal the day's radiance to the cold, slumbering city. On the horizon, the sun began the ascent to its throne, from where it would gaze at the peasants below.

The alarm buzzed purposefully, blaring its absurd melody in Lynaly's ears. She turned over, wincing at the abomination that beat her eardrums, and pulled the pillow over her head, trying to snuff out the incessant ruckus. Sheila lifted her head slightly, one eye peeking at the waking queen. Finally, Lynaly slammed her palm down upon the clock, silencing its mouth.

She sat up and momentarily allowed her feet to touch the cool carpet before heaving them back to the warm bed. She rubbed her eyes, contemplating withdrawing into the maw of the inviting bed. "Ugh, how could such a time of day be considered viable for 'education'? I suppose I've grown too accustomed to being nothing more than a spirit."

Sheila climbed to her feet and stretched her front legs, then hind. "*It is rather unconventional, isn't it? Soon, it won't matter all that much, will it?*" She peered up at Lynaly.

Lynaly scratched Sheila's ears and chin. "No, my sweet. Soon, it will not matter at all." She glanced at the tome on the nightstand. "Are you certain you are fine with this, my dear?"

Lynaly spoke to Lilly from the corner of her mind. "*We've had this discussion. I'll do whatever it takes. It'll be a process, I understand. But I remember the words. I know what I have to do.*"

"As long as you are aware of the risks," she said, stretching and standing. "There will be no turning back, Lynaly."

No response came from within.

"I'll take that as an acknowledgment."

After showering, Lynaly fitted herself with the preset ensemble, ensuring her appearance would startle everyone. Once fully dressed, she looked herself over.

She wore a short black-and-red plaid skirt, and her torso was engulfed in a black leather, silver-strapped corset to define her hips. Underneath the corset was a sheer white ruffled V-cut blouse that displayed her cleavage. On top, she wore an unzipped red leather mini jacket. Down her long legs ran black fishnet stockings. The cherry of it all as she adjusted her jewelry.

Sheila sat on the bed, her tail swishing back and forth atop the contorted comforter as Lynaly emerged from the bathroom. "*That looks exquisite. Quite suiting indeed.*"

Lynaly half-smiled. "Ah, but I am only partially done." She grabbed the pair of calf-high black-leather boots by the door and did them up, lace by lace, then sat down at the desk with a mirror. She powdered her face, further defining her already ghostly complexion. Next, she applied black eyeliner, eye shadow, and then cherry-red lipstick, which rendered her lips vibrant with the allure of a seductress. Once done, she brushed her hair, which flowed down her shoulders like the sun's rays.

"Perhaps we can change the color later—a darker shade would be much more suitable." Lynaly turned to Sheila. "Don't you think?"

Sheila blinked in agreement.

"*Once Sam is back, you can do whatever you want.*"

"My dear girl, it will be *us*, together, as one." Lynaly smiled at her bewitching reflection, which held a slightly sinister expression. "You will see when we complete the ritual and my power . . . becomes yours."

Satisfied with her appearance, she stood, gathered the tome and her belongings, and went to the door. Sheila ran to her side, and Lynaly placed her hands on her hips. "You'll have to wait outside until after it is done, you know that, right?"

"*I'd rather not,*" Sheila said, twitching her tail. "*Seeing as how dangerous it will be.*"

Lynaly just shook her head, and the two made their final trek from the hotel room.

They'd just missed the elevator. Lynaly sighed, and Sheila glanced up at her queen. "*Shame. To think they wouldn't hold the door.*"

Lynaly crouched to pet her. "Yes, I do hate waiting."

Soon, the doors parted, revealing an empty elevator. Lynaly entered. As Sheila followed, the door nearly closed on her tail, and she turned back and hissed, swatting at it. Lynaly grinned as she pressed the L button.

"Don't worry, my dear. Soon, we'll be in a much better place."

The lobby was bustling. At the front desk, she was greeted by Wilbur once again.

"Good morning, Ms. Sargent. How may I be of service?" Lynaly wanted to slap the stupid grin off his face.

"I will be checking out, Wilbur." Popping her hip, she placed the key on the desk.

She knew Wilbur had been studying her and had noted his nervousness since she stepped off the elevator. In fact, she could tell most of the people in the area were looking at her.

Wilbur opened his mouth, but all that came out was a squeak. Lynaly laughed in her head at the poor sap, who'd seemingly lost his marbles. He cleared his throat, obviously trying to constrict his voice so it sounded lower. "I trust your stay was pleasant, miss?"

Lynaly tossed her golden hair over her shoulder. "It was fine, nothing exceptional. Please charge the bill you have on my card. Hurry, I have somewhere to go."

Wilbur nodded. "Y-yes, miss. Right away."

Lynaly signed a receipt and then gave the jittery clerk a smile that seemed to melt him.

76

Soon, the duo was on the move again. As she walked through the lobby with Sheila, Lynaly was aware of the gazes—some bore shock, while others loomed with lust. As they neared the elevator to the parking garage, they crossed paths with a pair of teenage boys dressed in baggy clothing and practically salivating over her illustrious being. One of the boys motioned the cat to scram. The other knelt to pet Sheila.

Lynaly turned to him slowly. "I wouldn't do that if you know what's good for you."

The boy kneeling stopped in his tracks and looked up at Lynaly. "Why?"

She smirked. "She doesn't like strangers. You may want to leave now."

Sheila's black hair rose as she folded her ears back and growled at the sniveling pair of pigs—the boy standing laughed at the seemingly empty threat. In response, Sheila grew into her huntress form. The laughter quickly became a search for air.

In her overgrown shape, Sheila took a step toward her victims, who were retreating.

Lynaly smiled. "That will do, Sheila. I believe you've had your morning fun. Let's be grateful no one else saw this."

Sheila glanced back at Lynaly. "*Ah, I was only getting started.*"

In a cloud of black fog, Sheila reverted to her small form. Then Lynaly picked her up and called the elevator.

They once again walked past the scorch mark in the parking garage. This time, there was no sadness. Lynaly grinned.

Suddenly, feeling a familiar presence, she turned around. There were only cars and a subtle breeze wafted by.

Sheila's ears perked up, and she turned her nose to the breeze. "*I don't sense anything. Perhaps you're just anxious?*"

Lynaly sighed. "Maybe. It will be much easier when I know I can defend us properly. Come, my dear, we have much to do."

It was time to return to school—her first day in a long time. And indeed, her last.

CHAPTER 5

DRIVING THROUGH INGRAM'S CONGESTED streets, Lynaly was halted at every other red light and antagonized by the plentiful rude drivers. Above, the sky was free and clear, practically begging for the ants below to stare at its majesty.

At one light, lost in thoughts of the coming ritual and gazing at the wild blue yonder, Lynaly didn't notice when it turned green. A horn bellowed behind her. She glanced in her rearview mirror to see an older gentleman flailing his hands about. She remained where she was, and the light turned red again.

The gentleman's round face became as red as the exterior of his sports car. Lynaly grinned from ear to ear, watching his mouth flutter in a wild tantrum.

When the light turned green, Lynaly accelerated only slightly. The light soon turned to yellow and then red again. The red sports car swerved into the right lane, pulling alongside her.

The man was throwing vulgar words at an incredible rate, practically foaming at the mouth.

Lynaly sighed. "My word, such anger over driving. Truly, patience is not a virtue anymore."

"*You have no idea,*" said the girl within. "*Anger is spreading like wildfire.*"

On the passenger seat, Sheila yawned and stood to look at the vile man. "*I don't suppose you'll let this ingrate off easy, are you?*"

Lynaly grinned malevolently and revved her engine.

Sheila cocked her head. "*Racing? Isn't that reckless?*"

The man eagerly gripped his steering wheel, waiting for the light to change.

"Just watch. You'll see what's in store for our fine friend here."

Sheila snickered and stuck out her tongue at the vile red beast—its make and color were unpleasantly familiar to her mind's inhabitant.

The light flickered to green, and the sports car's rear tires spun in place for a few seconds. Lynaly slowly accelerated and watched the red demon speed off.

"Wait for it . . ." Lynaly grinned.

A police cruiser emerged behind a line of stopped cars at the intersection to her right. Flying out into the street, red, white, and blue lights flashing, it gave chase. Soon, the red terror was out of sight.

As Lynaly got closer to the school, she slowed in a congested area—a red sports car had lost control and smashed into a tree. Emergency response vehicles littered the road's shoulder. Lynaly caught sight of a stretcher being rushed to an ambulance. She grinned as she noticed the man's dazed eyes on it. His bloodied face turned red again.

)

The eventful drive was complete, and Lynaly pulled into Ingram High School's parking lot. A sign in the student parking area of the lot read UNDER CONSTRUCTION, and equipment littered the space. Lynaly reached the staff parking area and found a spot near the building's entrance. A campus security guard approached the car as Lynaly was about to exit.

"Excuse me, miss, you can't park here."

She rolled down the window. "Check the staff sticker on the window if you want. My parents were the Sargents. Mona and Johnny Sargent."

A moment passed, and then the guard nodded. "Sorry. It's no problem. Have a good day."

Lynaly exited the vehicle and scanned the area for threats but saw only students. Sheila jumped out as well, ignoring her mistress's earlier command. Also searching for threats, Sheila turned up her nose and growled. Lynaly patted her companion on the head. "There, there, my sweet. They wouldn't dare attack in the open. If you will join me, do so from a distance."

She slowly made her way through the lot. Sheila slinked behind her. Students clustered in groups, many in the front area around the old statue—the Deupree Watchtower of Ingram. All eyes were glued to the girl who strutted past them. The men drooled, both students and faculty, while the women glared with a burning passion. Lynaly stifled a laugh.

"*Jealous prudes, infelicitous men. The surroundings may have evolved, but humanity has not. Typical.*"

Discussions about the girl's identity and where she came from began circulating. Lynaly continued her trek toward the two pairs of open doors, enjoying the chatter.

Ingram High School was shoddy on the outside. Built in the 1970s, it was renovated to remove contaminated materials and satisfy building codes. The exterior was composed of dull, lifeless gray brick. Inside was a different story. The walls were glossy red on top and glossy white on the bottom. New lockers had been installed, though many were already soiled with graffiti.

Students watched the unknown nobody float through the hallway. Behind Lynaly, Sheila had begun her infiltration mission, sticking to the shadows as much as possible.

Lynaly searched her mind, trying to determine where the administrative office was to sign up for the talent show. As she was doing so, a group of girls approached. All wore disgusted looks. The apparent leader of the group chewed a piece of gum obnoxiously.

Oh, man. It's Beth. I really wish she hadn't seen us.

"*Don't worry, dear. It will all work out.*"

Beth was the "popular girl." She could do no wrong, and with the curves of an hourglass, the bosom of a Barbie doll, and legs that went on for days, she had almost everyone wrapped around her finger. Her long platinum-blonde hair framed her smooth, round face with high cheekbones. Her eyes were bright blue—obviously adorned with contacts. The sound of her high heels on the tile reminded Lynaly of deer hooves. She wore a tight leather miniskirt that was way too short, a sheer white blouse that showed off ample cleavage, and a white lace bra that was visible through the blouse. Lynaly gazed upon her with a shiver of revulsion.

Beth smirked. "What's the matter, sweetheart? See something ya like?" She flipped her hair dramatically.

Lynaly smiled. "I'd like to figure out what the hell you're wearing, then shower and get tested for diseases."

Beth's followers looked at each other, awed by the slew of words directed at their fearless leader.

The girl's face turned red. "Honey, have you checked yourself in the mirror? I wouldn't talk, and if you know what's good for you, you'll hold your tongue around me."

Lynaly stepped toward Beth, allowing the magenta glow to flicker in her vibrant green eyes. She leaned in to whisper in Beth's ear. "If you know what's good for you, you'll start running away now . . . *sweetheart.*"

With that, Lynaly continued walking down the hallway while Beth stood in shock. The other girls huddled around her.

"What did she say?"

"Did you see her eyes? Oh my God, they're gorgeous!"

"Like, really, did you see her outfit? Oh my God, it was so cute!"

"She's kinda creepy."

Beth clenched her fists. "Shut up!" She turned around and glared down the hall at Lynaly, who stopped. She turned her head to meet Beth's gaze and gave her a wicked smile.

Beth shuddered.

)

Shane closed his locker and came face-to-face with the cocky grin of his friend and classmate Steve. He jumped slightly.

Steve laughed. Like Shane, Steve was tall, had black hair, and had an athletic build. Physically, the two could have passed as brothers, but Steve was far more of an annoyance, an instigator, whereas Shane was more reserved.

"Jesus, Steve, I told you to stop doing that shit."

Steve laughed harder. "You're such a pussy, I swear. Are you sure your balls have dropped? I mean, damn, Shane." He bent over and retied a loose shoelace on his white high-top sneakers. "Don't be checking out my ass either."

"Don't worry, if I were, I'd have already contracted the clap."

Steve stood up. "Cute. I like a witty one."

Shane rolled his eyes. "Who's the sexually repressed one now?"

This time, they both laughed. As they headed down the hall, both received occasional disgusted glances from girls.

"So, we still gonna do what we planned?" Steve said. "Today's the day, you know."

Shane hesitated. "Ah, man, I don't know."

Steve stopped and forced Shane to follow suit. They stood amid the busy school highway.

"C'mon, Shane, don't pussy out on this. We're graduating—let's leave our mark! Make the underclassmen remember us." He gripped his friend's shoulder.

As Shane glanced around the hallway, trying to decide what to do, he saw a girl stepping out of the administration office. She met his gaze and began walking his way.

He squinted. *Is that Lynaly? She looks so different from her usual lively self.* He supposed that everything she'd been through recently had taken its toll on her. *I wish I'd gotten to know—*

"The hell's the matter? Shane?" Steve looked down the hallway. "Oh. Damn!"

As Lynaly approached, Shane's face turned a few shades of red. "H-hey, Lyn. I'm really sorry about your parents—and Sam."

Lynaly gave him a small smile. "Thank you, Shane."

Steve cleared his throat. "So. Yeah. I know we've never really been close friends, but . . . I want you to know that if you ever need me . . . or anything, just ask, OK?"

Still smiling, Lynaly leaned in close to Shane and spoke quietly. "Leave here today and forget about me." After giving him a peck on his cheek, she proceeded to walk away.

Steve frowned. "What the hell was that all about? What did she say to you?"

Shane was bewildered. *Leave?* He puzzled over the statement until Steve socked him in the shoulder. "Ow! What the fuck, man?"

"Come on, daydreamer," Steve said, looking giddy with anticipation. "Let's get her at the show."

Shane shook his head. "I don't know. Kicking her while she's down after what's happened? I think we should just skip for the day. Something feels wrong."

Steve just rolled his eyes, but Shane's gut writhed with uneasiness. Something was going to happen. He could feel it.

)

Soon, the talent show was underway. Many students had come to display the skills they would pursue to success—or die trying—and the auditorium was bustling with *shhs*, foot taps, and make-outs.

Wanting to be in a convenient place when she was called, Lynaly had taken a seat in the first row. The new seats were covered in maroon cloth and allowed for adequate reclining, a valuable feature for those students "experimenting" with each other.

The floor was made of cold black marble with hints of white. The walls stretched high, and grand, and a magnificent chandelier hung from the ceiling. It glowed dimly as the various acts performed before the masses.

Some told jokes or stories, some played instruments and confessed their love for each other, and on and on. Then, it was time for the high school's well-known band, Woman's Potion. The origin of the name was unknown, but they were definitely an act to watch. A voice welcomed them to the stage, and as the band members clambered out from behind the parting curtain, the student body roared into a frenzy. They played several original songs, then finished with covers of the Misfits' "Descending Angel" and Chicago's "If You Leave Me Now."

Lynaly rolled her eyes. "*Anything to please the audience, I suppose.*"

It is almost time, my dear. Are you prepared?

"*I'm ready. Today, we become one. To get Sam back!*"

Another malevolent grin spread across Lynaly's face.

)

The moment had come. The stage cleared. The room was silent.

"And now, everyone. Please give a warm welcome to Lynaly Sargent!"

At that moment, Lilly gave up her possession of Lynaly's body and retreated to her psyche.

"*You will be the one to complete the ritual, my dear.*"

There was light applause, but when the crowd saw the mystery girl take the stage and realized they'd known her all along, the room roared with whistles and chatter. Standing before everyone in front of the closed curtains, the lights of the auditorium shining upon her angelic face, radiant golden locks, and emerald green eyes, Lynaly was a sight to behold. A sight indeed.

For a moment, darkness filled the auditorium. Behind the swaying crimson drapes, two boys huddled together with eggs. In their seats, students looked on in anticipation. Some grew restless, stirring, longing, their eyes hungry to feast upon the spectacle.

Then the spotlight flickered on, revealing the beauty that entranced the now silent auditorium. She beamed a smile as brilliant as the light that shone on her. Beneath her, her shadow stretched across the floor and curtain.

The boys remained patiently behind the curtain, plotting, unaware that this day wouldn't just go down in the school's history but humankind's.

Lynaly's mouth opened. As her mind recalled words, her angelic voice recited them. Jaws dropped, and spectators were roused to their feet like sailors being beckoned to their doom by a siren.

Her task was nearly complete.

In the shadows, Steve nudged Shane. "Now! Let's get her now!"

"I-I don't know, man. I mean . . . listen to her," Shane said, more reluctant than ever to disturb Lynaly's performance.

"Dude, grow some balls! We're going to go down in history, man! Think of all the chicks we'll get from this!" Steve made an obscene jerking motion.

"All right, let's get this over quickly."

Flinging open the curtain, they sprinted onto the stage and threw the eggs at Lynaly. "Gotcha!"

A voice boomed over the speaker. "Stop! Get off the stage!"

Still, Lynaly sang, ignoring the disturbance. The shade beneath her grew and wrapped around her feet and legs.

Shane and Steve stopped dead, still behind her.

Then Lynaly spun around, continuing to sing her siren melody. The shade grew massive, enshrouding her.

"You like to play tricks, do you?" boomed a seductive and foreboding voice. "Well, I have a trick for you."

The shade burst forth, consuming Steve wholly, ridding him of his flesh and bones and leaving only ash. His screams were immediately erased into nothingness.

"Gotcha!" the voice cackled maniacally as the spectators shrieked in horror.

Attention returned to the audience. "The show has only begun, my friends. Please be seated!"

The shade burst forth again from the once angelic, awe-inspiring girl. Shadowy blades swirled around the room, chopping up bodies and then devouring the souls, which were drained into the dark void beneath Lynaly. Blood and various body parts splattered the maroon seats. Screams flooded the room amid the twisted, hideous cackle.

And center stage, Hell manifested on Earth.

Flames emerged from the gaping void, and soon, a wildfire spread from the stage to the rows of seats.

Slowly, the shade turned back toward a horrified Shane, frozen in place. "You. I have a special place for you. Open your heart for me, won't you?"

"No, *save him, Lilly! He's of no harm.*"

"As you wish, dear, but I must remind you that I have no control over the avatar."

For a moment, the shade seemed restrained by an invisible force. Lynaly knew it was Lilly attempting to hold the phantasm with her magic.

Taking the opportunity, Lynaly let her inner voice be heard. "*I told you to leave! Run now! I can't hold it for long!*"

Shane scrambled to his senses and fled through the backstage door.

As the fire consumed the student body's remains, the avatar separated itself from Lynaly's body and began to bubble and swirl. Lynaly continued to sing, still lost in her trance.

Another roar echoed throughout the space, shaking the auditorium's foundation. The shade twisted and molded itself into a figure. Flames merged with the blackness, and flesh, blood, bone, and ash swirled in the storm. Slowly but surely, the shade took on its final form—one Lynaly hadn't expected.

It was the test she'd been warned about.

She stopped singing. The shade had completed its transformation, having absorbed more than enough matter to achieve its manifestation. It knelt before her in a makeshift, tattered ash robe. Its eyes were blue, its face square and dotted with stubble, and its hair short and dark brown. It gazed up at its summoner.

"Lynaly . . ."

Lynaly rubbed her eyes. "S-Sam? Sam, is it you?"

"*Do not be fooled!*" Lilly pleaded. "*It is a test, Lynaly, a safeguard to ensure you fail in bonding with me! The biggest part of your heart has manifested before you, and they will use your love for Sam against you!*"

"It's Sam, though. How can I kill Sam?"

He smiled. "I can't believe it, Lynaly. I'm really back. You did it."

She embraced him, sobbing. "I've missed you so much."

Lilly raged in Lynaly's mind. "*Stupid girl! You'll get yourself killed! Don't let your guard down!*"

"I've missed you too, Lynaly," Sam whispered. "I'm so sorry . . ."

Lynaly sniffled. "For what?"

He pulled back and raised a bone scythe over his head. "You should have listened to her!"

Lynaly fell backward as he drove the scythe toward her. Missing her, it passed through him instead.

"Meddlesome gnat! You dare dabble in magic far beyond your comprehension! Lilith's release into this world will spell certain doom!"

Sam's face transformed into a skull. Jagged edges protruded from its pointed chin, and fiery eyes blazed in the skull's sockets.

Lynaly felt a chill run up her spine.

"*Use the knowledge you read to defend yourself.*"

Lynaly quickly remembered several passages from the musty old tome and thought of Lilly's wisdom when she wore the earrings, choker, and ring.

Another roaring voice raged through the fast-falling auditorium—Sam's. "*You will not dare harm her. Lynaly, it's not me! Get away from it now! It's only trying to trick you into thinking it's me.*"

Just then, Sheila leaped onto the stage before the ash-enshrouded tyrant.

The avatar gazed down upon the pathetic-looking feline and laughed. "Begone! You are of no importance, pest. Unless you have a death wish—I would be happy to fulfill it!"

Enraged, Sheila burst into her huntress form. "*I will tear you limb from limb, fiend!*"

The skull glowed bright red and orange. "So be it."

Sheila lunged at the avatar, and they both rolled across the stage and crashed into a pillar, causing the auditorium's top level to cave in on them. Smoke billowed into the outside world as sunlight poured in.

"No! Sam!" Lynaly cried out.

The rubble shifted, and then the massive avatar flung Sheila across the stage. "You challenged death, and so you shall have it!" the monster roared.

Lynaly clenched her fists. "No! Not today!" She reached for a shard of broken glass and sliced her upper arms. Droplets of blood ran down them, and when the blood reached her hands, she clapped them together. Her earrings, choker, and ring glowed fiery red. In her hands, she now held a flame. The blood boiled in her veins and dried up on her arms and hands.

The monster roared with laughter. "You'll need something more than a little flame, witch."

"I've only just begun." Lynaly smiled as the flame became white, then blue. She could feel all Lilly's rage, sorrow, despair, and sadness in her hands, quadrupling in size, releasing itself into her fingertips.

Then, she hurled it at the monster before her with all her might. Lightning flickered through its body.

"No! It cannot be. I cannot die! I am immortal!" The monster shrieked and wailed as it began to shrink. "If I am to die, I'll take you with me!"

At that, the shade hurled its massive scythe at Lynaly.

She cringed, but the blow never came. She slowly opened her eyes to find Sheila standing before her, the scythe in her mouth.

"I believe this is yours," the huntress told the monster. Then she darted across the stage and plunged the scythe deep into its gut before mauling what remained to shreds—back to the flesh, bone, and blood from whence it had come.

"It is done. You have done well, my dear Lynaly."

"Is it time?" Lynaly asked. Pain radiated down her arms, and she collapsed to the ground in shock.

Sheila lifted her gently with her mouth and flung her onto her back.

)

Deep in the burning auditorium, a victim clung to life under the corpses of classmates and friends. Her eyes were red with tears of blood, her skin becoming between a state of pale and gray, while her lips were envenomed with a vengeance.

No, not yet. I will get you, Lynaly.

)

In the woods behind the school, far from prying eyes, Sheila set Lynaly down on the ground. "How are you?" asked Sam, who still existed within the feline.

Carefully, Lynaly stood and examined her hands and feet. "Finally . . ." Then she addressed the girl within. "You still exist, my dear. This is still your body. But now, I am in control. You will start seeing things more my way.

"Lilly, *why hasn't Sam returned?*" the girl asked, peering outside from deep within. "*I thought the ritual would bring him back?*"

"My child, to truly bring Sam back, we will require magic greater than a simple incantation. Mind you, this was no mere spell—you are now bonded with me. But we'll be needing something stronger, and I know just the thing . . . and place. That won't be a problem now, will it?"

"*I agreed to it, didn't I?*" she muttered.

"I'm sure we can institute weekend visitation—if that would suit you." The humor was met with a subtle chuckle from within. "You are, however, Lynaly no more, for you are me, and I am you." A breeze passed by, carrying the scent of ash and flesh. "It's time to leave this place."

Sheila had reverted to her compact form, and she stayed close as they returned to the school parking lot in hopes of obtaining the white sedan unnoticed.

"*I think you should still use my name. Lynaly.*"

"Yes, better for blending in." She smiled. "Lynaly. Lynaly Sargent."

)

Mayhem was all about the schoolyard. Fire engines, police cars, ambulances, and people were scattered throughout the space.

As Lynaly drove up to the exit, a police officer stopped her. She rolled down her window.

"Ma'am," he said, his voice deep and stern. "Were you in the building today?"

"No, sir," she said softly. "I just arrived to pick up my homework and saw the damage. I skipped classes today because a friend is sick, and I wanted to check on her."

"All right," he said, waving her on. "Move along."

Soon, she'd reached the interstate that led out of Ingram, and before she knew it, the city was miles behind her. In her rearview mirror, the sky was a hazy yellow, broken by a lone black pillar of smoke and ash. The road into the city was congested, but the road out was clear.

Lynaly was no longer herself but Lilith. She existed as a thought, a piece of a subconscious able to be brought forth as needed. Lilith would always be present, and she was at her mercy.

Lilith grinned, already enjoying the change—the freedom. Oh, *the places we'll go and the hell we will raise.*

)

Where am I? Why can't I move?

Beth's thoughts drifted in the abysmal sea of the void. She felt numb to the cold, like her body had long since given up on sensation. She didn't float or sit—she just . . . existed. At least, she thought she did.

Emotions rippled like waves in the emptiness: rage, sadness, and love—emotions that began to manifest before her like a cruel performance. Something was drawing her back to a happy memory: the prom, Brian, and all that was stolen from her.

But why?

A soft white light began to emanate above her, gradually growing brighter as hues of violet and blue waltzed around its edges. Then, suddenly, a familiar voice pierced the silence.

"Hey, dummy? You alright there?" Brian's warm and familiar voice broke through.

Beth blinked, her vision coming into focus. She was seated in a dark plastic chair, the muted strains of prom music in the background, and Brian stood beside her in a crisp royal blue tuxedo, a paper cup of fruit punch in his hand.

"Huh? What?" she replied, stretching lazily as the night's festive energy tugged at her senses.

"Are you gonna dance with me at our prom or sleep all night?" Brian grinned, nudging her playfully.

For a moment, a genuine smile crept onto Beth's face. But then, an inexplicable heaviness settled over her, an unsettling feeling that something was amiss. She glanced around the banquet hall. The lights, laughter, and the gentle hum of conversation all felt too perfect . . . too staged.

As her eyes roamed the room, they fell upon a solitary figure in the far corner, a young woman shrouded in an eerie, almost imperceptible magenta glow. At first, it seemed small, like a distant ember, but then it spread, creeping outward like wildfire, setting the edges of Beth's vision ablaze. Beth's stomach churned. "Who's that?" she whispered urgently.

Brian looked puzzled. "Who?"

"There was a girl in the corner . . . she was right there," Beth insisted, her voice trembling as she clutched at the edge of her chair. "It's like there's something pure evil radiating from her."

Brian frowned, glancing around. "Beth, you're shaking. Are you sure you saw someone? Maybe it was just the lights."

Before she could answer, the atmosphere in the hall warped. It was all wrong. The music slowed, warping into overlapping echoes of screams. Shadows stretched and twisted across the floor, and the gentle lighting pulsated like a frantic heartbeat.

Then, the world cracked open: the prom and auditorium merged into a nightmarish kaleidoscope. Beth stumbled, struggling to keep her footing. She reached for a table, her hand slipping on something wet and warm. She stared in horror as everyone around her was slaughtered. Beth's heart hammered as the once-happy scene became a vortex of horror: students screamed, their skin splitting, eyes wide in terror; bodies collapsed in grotesque piles as if some unseen force were harvesting life itself.

Beth's vision blurred for a moment before locking eyes with the magenta figure at the center of that commotion. Lynaly stood there as flames danced along her arms, with her alluring and merciless smile. "So, have you remembered, dear puppet?" Lynaly cooed, her voice echoing over the chaos.

Beth's voice cracked with anguish, "You killed them . . . you killed everyone!"

Lynaly tilted her head, a cruel smile playing on her lips. "Did I, or did I merely reveal what was always inside you? Better yet, why don't you return to *your* world, dear little Beth."

First, Beth was dumbstruck, and then came everything else: grief and searing anger. She surged forward. She lunged at Lynaly, but as her hand reached out, it was all for naught; a torrent of fire engulfed her. The pain was instantaneous and all-consuming.

Is this it? Is this how I die? Again? Beth thought, the horror mingling with a desperate, primal fury.

Then, a new voice, cold and mocking, whispered through the inferno within her mind, "No, *little one. If you agree, you can exact your revenge, or you can perish for all of eternity. This can be where you begin.*"

The choice was made unbeknownst to Beth, for her soul knew. An immense pressure bore down on her chest, like unseen hands forcing her to submit, squeezing until she thought her ribs might crack.

With a final, shuddering cry, the fire subsided, replaced by an oppressive, biting cold. Beth felt an overwhelming emptiness, as if the very essence of her was being stripped away. Cat's eyes scanned through these memories, relishing in the bargain gained and the impending freedom that awaited not only Beth . . . but *her.* However, something was wrong—perhaps a twist of fate—something that even the Order and all their supposed years of wisdom could not see coming. Yes. The last feeling she clung to was Brian, and the last thing she had heard him say was, "Stay with me." And that ignited a spark.

"*You have made a sagacious choice, my dear. Now then, let's give you that wake-up call,*" said the voice.

And then, in a brutal rupture, the plastic body bag that had contained her fell apart with a sharp, tearing sound—like the breaking of a chrysalis in the dead of night.

Beth emerged onto the cold floor of the collapsed mobile morgue, her body battered and raw. The stench of rot and charred flesh assaulted her senses. The scattered remnants of her classmates surrounded her—disjointed limbs, shattered glass, and the echo of a life that had once been. Yet, amid the ruins, a sinister calm settled over her.

The voice, velvet-smooth and dripping with disdain, whispered inside her: "*Now that you've made the choice, we have work to do.*"

Beth could sense the hint of a mile-wide grin from this . . . entity. It felt like eyes were watching her, unseen yet omnipresent, as though something lurked just beyond the veil of reality, observing her with a cruel curiosity. That presence in the void had sealed her fate with one crushing, inescapable blow.

"*Let's get you patched up so we can begin. . .*" An orange light emanated around her. Black leather clothes, boots, and a heavy, black woolen robe manifested on her body. She didn't notice, nor would she have cared, about the faint religious symbols stitched into the back of the robe—what mattered was that she had been claimed, and what *really* mattered was that *bitch* was going to pay and pay big. Beth's blood pounded in her ears, not with fear, but with a fierce, unyielding rage.

"Right," she murmured, her voice echoing softly into the shattered night. Let's go hunting."

CHAPTER 6

SHANE JOLTED AWAKE, SWEAT clinging to his skin, breath ragged and uneven. The dream still played in his head—the screams, the blood, the bodies crumpled like discarded dolls. He had seen Steve die in front of him again, just like that day. Only this time, Lynaly's eyes glowed with something beyond human as when she spared him.

Why? Why did she let him live? His heart pounded against his ribs, and his fingers dug into the damp sheets. A whisper of movement in the dark sent a shiver down his spine. His body tensed. Someone else was here.

"You've seen a glimpse of the other side, and now you don't know what to do with it." The voice was smooth, deliberate, and alarmingly close.

Shane's breath caught in his throat as his eyes darted around. A pair of red eyes, glowing like embers, flickered in the corner of the room. A shrouded figure stepped into the pale moonlight that filtered through his window. The man's right hand glowed eerily—a soft, ever-shifting red. Shane couldn't tell if it was gloved, bare skin, or something else entirely, but the sight of it made his stomach twist.

The man held up his hands. "I'm not here to hurt you, young one," the man said, his voice laced with amusement. "I am merely here to offer . . . clarity. Life's paths often diverge unexpectedly, and you stand at one such crossroads."

Shane forced himself to sit up, his limbs heavy. "Who—who are you?" His throat was dry. "What do you want?"

The man let out a low chuckle. "On the contrary, I was human. Once. A long time ago." He lifted his red right hand, turning it over slowly as if inspecting it himself. "Time is a fickle, fluid thing. It can be made, broken, and rewritten in ways most minds cannot comprehend."

The air in the room shifted—the walls felt closer, the dark corners stretching outward. A pressure built behind Shane's eyes, like something unseen was pressing in on him.

"The one who killed your classmates. . ." The man's voice took on a soft, contemplative tone. "I know them well, and I know what's coming. That is to say, what has been coming for a long, longtime." He turned his head slightly toward the window, where the faint glow of headlights reflected off the glass. "*They* are watching you."

Shane followed his gaze, his breath catching in his throat. A police car sat outside, unmoving, watching. His stomach twisted again.

"The cops?"

The man smirked, amused. "No. Not them. They're just men doing their job, searching for answers to something they'll never fully understand." His red right hand curled slightly. "But the real danger? Ah, that lies elsewhere."

Shane's pulse thundered in his ears. "What do they want with me?"

"Simple—to claim you or have you erased," the man said bluntly. "That is their nature."

Shane clenched his fists. "That's not much of a choice."

The Man with the Red Right Hand turned to him, his smile widening in the moonlight. "It never is."

)

Morning came, and with it, chores. Mourning would have to continue to wait as always because, after all, life goes on.

"Shane, honey. Can you take out the trash and put it down by the curb for tomorrow?" his mom asked.

"Sure, Mom," he replied.

He exited the house, put the two trash bags in the dumpster, and started wheeling the bins down the driveway. Shane considered the terms of the deal he was offered. It felt too good to be true, and he remembered that if it sounded and seemed too good to be true, it likely was. He was

The sun radiated warmth, soothing his body. It was a quiet day in the neighborhood... or so he thought until...

Two detectives appeared: one tall and thin, the other tall but overweight, finishing up a doughnut.

"Shane Bridget?" the tall one asked.

"Ye—yeah?"

The pair flashed their badges. "Detective Stickler, and this is my partner, Detective Cromwell. Can we ask you a few questions?"

Shane recalled the Man with the Red Right Hand's warning: *The real danger lies somewhere else* . . . Then he thought back on who and what the Order was, and by the man's cautionary tale. *He said they were fine* . . . *right?* He dismissed it and tried giving the two the benefit of the doubt.

"I am not sure I can be of much help, but sure, I can try."

The larger detective took a sip of his coffee. "Great, thanks for your cooperation, kid. This won't take long."

Some time had passed as the duo grilled the young man.

Shane thought, *This is starting to feel like an interrogation, more than a simple question.* He could sense his blood beginning to boil.

"Look, I've told you everything I know and what happened. There was a fire—something went wrong with the electrical system during a performance, and by then, I had already run," Shane said, hoping they'd buy it and leave it at that.

"I dunno, kid," Detective Stickler said. "How the hell do kids get chopped up like that in a blender? There were reports of a girl straight-up butchering people."

Detective Cromwell tapped Stickler's shoulder. "We need to wrap this up." Something—or rather, someone—caught his eye down the street. "Something's fishy with that van."

The trio turned their attention and saw a group of men enter a white van and sit at attention, almost waiting for something.

"This . . . does not look well," said Stickler. "Alright, kid, the interview's over. Go back inside and lock the door." Shane slowly backed away and walked to his house. Stickler motioned to his partner, "Call in dispatch and bring the car up; I'm going to have a little walk."

"Just don't do anything stupid, like you normally do, OK?" replied Cromwell as he returned to his car.

Shane had gone upstairs to his house and peeked out the window to see the van speeding down the street, with the duo giving chase.

He could leave. He should leave. But now he knew that whatever the Order was, they wouldn't let him go that easily. He realized that he would need to be . . . something more.

)

The air was thick with the scent of incense and burning wax. Massive black candles lined the chamber walls, while roaring braziers cast long, dancing shadows that seemed to slither across the stone floor. Deep in the heart of the earth, the High Chamber of the Order was a place of both reverence and fear. The council sat in a semicircle of ancient thrones, towering above the dark altar where Atreyu approached.

From the far left wing, seated like a vulture on his throne, Albedo watched with a faint smirk as though he knew something Atreyu did not. He had suspected the snake was trying to undermine him—and the Master. The fool thought he went unnoticed. He was wrong.

Atreyu knelt, head bowed, eyes closed. He could feel their gazes—still judging, still measuring. For all his cunning, he knew better than to show hesitation here. But still, a faint unease lingered . . . as if some other unseen force watched him even now, waiting, plotting.

"Master, I am at your command."

"Rise, Atreyu," came a voice from the darkness—smooth, commanding, and ancient—the Master of the Order. Atreyu knew and served him well.

Atreyu rose and gave a grand bowing gesture.

"Yes, your Excellency, the vessel offered no resistance," Atreyu replied, smiling like a proud parent.

"Good." Atreyu could detect a hint of a smile in the darkness before him. "That tool will be an instrument in keeping that harlot in check," the Master said sharply.

"But of course, your Excellency, everything is coming together. I am pleased to say that, that tool is on its way—" Atreyu was interrupted by another member of the Order.

"We don't care about 'plans coming together.' We want results!"

"Yes! Results determine our path of righteousness!" Quipped another.

"It's your fault that *witch* was able to get back out into the world in the first place. Your safeguard failed, and now we've more work to do because of it!" said Albedo.

Rage flickered in Atreyu for a split second to shift the flames that danced in the High Chamber. He did well to hide it behind his mask.

"Of course, Albedo. As you did, I underestimated that *witch*, as you so put it; the error is mine, and mine alone. Though I think my results thus far have more than spoken for themselves." Atreyu replied condescendingly.

"Insolence! You dare speak back to me in that tone?" cried Albedo, slamming his fist down on his throne.

A thunderous boom echoed throughout the chambers. "Enough!" The Master let out a sigh. "Atreyu has been loyal to our service for almost as long as you have, Albedo. I think his plans warrant praise."

"But your Excellency, perhaps your judgment is clouded because he may be of fam—"

The Master let loose another thunderous boom that shook the very core of the temple. "You would do well not to finish that sentence, Albedo."

"Apologies, sir." Albedo recoiled like a scolded puppy and silenced.

"Now, then. Atreyu. . ." The dark-shrouded figure swirled and appeared as a holy light before him. Atreyu bowed. A hand reached out and was placed on his shoulder. Other members gasped at the rare public gesture while Albedo's eyes darkened with unspoken disgust. "The detectives," the Master said coldly. "I want you to deal with them. Permanently."

Atreyu bowed his head lower, hiding his smile. "As you wish, your Excellency."

And yet, he couldn't shake the feeling that up until tonight, something was . . . different. He began to wonder if there had been something he missed. It was true; all the pieces were falling into place as he envisioned it . . . but not all of them were his. After the Master departed, vanishing through a portal of swirling darkness, Atreyu rose, smoothing his robes.

He thought for a brief moment about his strategy and what he should do next before being interrupted.

"*Master Atreyu,*" a voice piped into his mind.

"*Speak.*"

"*I've found it, sir. What Albedo was hiding.*"

Atreyu glanced at Albedo's way, and a slow, mile-wide smile crossed his face. At last, *the final nail needed to be put in that old buffoon's coffin!*

"Excellent work, Soevian."

Without a word, Atreyu turned, his smile lingering as he left the chamber, already savoring the long-awaited ascension ahead. Still, he needed to be cautious; the old dog had plenty of tricks, but he considered himself craftier. Then, a wild idea came to his mind: how to use that newly acquired piece. Ah, *I know . . . let's try out that polymorph spell.* Atreyu left the High Chamber with a pep in his step, whistling, before smirking at the thought of the inevitable future. *Once he's out of the way, it's just two hands and an old man to deal with before it's all mine.*

Similarly, Albedo scoffed at the man-child, and a smirk crept across as he realized the fly he believed to have caught. *I've got you right where I want you, boy.*

)

Blue and white flames consumed the parchment, leaving behind a scent that stung his senses. The candle flickered, casting long, crooked shadows against Shane's bedroom walls. Though now gone from sight, the contract burned in his mind—inked with his blood, sealed with words he could barely understand, and the man's counsel was cryptic, like a monkey's paw.

The Man with the Red Right Hand stood just beyond the edge of the light, watching with slight amusement. There was an eerie calm about him, a predator's patience, a cat toying with a mouse.

"You hesitate," the man said softly, breaking the silence. "You wonder if you made a mistake."

Shane sat cross-legged on his bed, hands trembling. "I didn't say that."

"You didn't have to." The man stepped forward, the crimson hue of his right hand casting a faint, otherworldly glow over the room. "Regret is the weight of the living. The dead have no such burden."

"What exactly do you want from me?" Shane asked, voice hoarse.

The Man with the Red Right Hand stood beside the bed, gazing at him with unsettling intensity. "Only what you already know, young one. You are a piece on the board—whether you fight or run, you *will* be moved. What matters is *how* you move—and *who* you move for."

A flicker of something human passed across the man's face, not warmth, but perhaps recognition of Shane's fear.

"You stood in the massacre and lived," the man said more quietly. "You think that was an accident? No. That was design."

Shane shivered. The images of the school, the fire, the bodies, Steve, Lynaly . . . they all came rushing back.

"You were spared for a reason," the man said, almost gently now. "And I suspect you will soon understand what that reason was."

The silence was deafening between the two, but for all his cryptic nuances, the man before him never once lied, and he felt deep down that it was *he*—who had far more to lose than Shane. He thought on the man's words.

"Regret is the weight of the living, huh? Fine." His eyes met with the twin embers that flickered. "I will do what I can for my part, but I need reassurance."

The pale face and embers nodded. "Of course, I will do all that I can. In the beginning, you'll grasp the powers slowly and, over time, learn to use them properly. Think of it as a form of mental training."

Shane sighed. "This is already making my head hurt," he said.

The Man with the Red Right Hand grinned like an amused schoolteacher. "But at least you're alive and can live on, fight to honor your friends' memories, and in turn, help save the world."

)

On the right side of the road there was a sign that read, "Welcome to Middleton, Founded 1728." Lynaly and Sheila had reached their destination. They were in Massachusetts.

Lynaly drove through the quiet town. Dawn would make its appearance shortly. At last, she pulled up the long driveway to the large house, whose shape reminded her of a witch's hat. The moon smiled, and the stars seemed to rejoice at the relocation.

She carried her things up the black-cherry steps guarded by two gargoyles, Sheila close behind her.

Hours later, she awoke on the couch. Sun flooded the main level. At her feet, Sheila was sprawled in a contorted state. She gathered and headed to the bathroom, leaving the slumbering feline purring.

The massive space offered a jet tub, two shower stalls, and a French ivory clawfoot bathtub. In the corner were two toilets with a divider between them. Classic black-and-white tile adorned the floor.

It was time to apply the hair dye.

Afterward, she showered, toweled herself off, and wrapped herself in a white robe that hung invitingly on a rack. Wiping steam off the mirror above one of the French ivory sinks, she leaned forward to examine the black strands of hair—Lynaly's, now her own.

She smiled. "Only the beginning."

Once clothed, she returned to the living room. It was time to tackle other matters. "I suppose if I am to blend in, I will need a job, right?" she said aloud.

"Yes, *that would be wise.*"

"Very well. Let's see here . . ."

Spotting the newspaper on the front step, she retrieved it and set about checking the classifieds.

"Ah. 'Looking for an energetic individual for Romero's Theater. Apply in person.' It seems like that's the ticket." Lynaly grinned and called Sheila. "Let's go."

)

A beaten-up brown 1971 Oldsmobile Delta 88 sedan pulled up alongside them at a stoplight. Lynaly looked to her right to see a slightly obese man with square-rimmed glasses and a scruffy face. To his right was a man with dark brown hair and a broad face. Dark circles hung under his eyes.

She retracted her gaze as he glanced over, unable to keep the malevolent grin off her face. "After all these years, at long last. I've found him."

"*Who is that?*" Sheila asked.

"My dear, *that* is the man who betrayed me, along with my dear brother, Atreyu."

Sheila blinked. "*Something about him is familiar. Like I'm staring at a mirror.*"

Lynaly ran her fingers down the cat's back. "Must be a coincidence," she replied, withholding only information she knew about the man. "The other one, however. He could be a problem."

Sheila stared. "*What do you mean?*"

"There's something about him that seems . . . off. Pure. Think nothing of it." She smiled at Sheila.

The light turned green, and the cars parted ways.

)

High atop Middleton's lone sentinel, Atreyu watched as his sister drove away in a brown car. A slight laugh escaped him, carried away by the winds that ushered in an approaching storm.

"So, she's found him—and so soon," he mused.

He then turned his gaze to another part of town, where a goth girl strolled along the streets, unaware of the gift she possessed. "Ah, what's this? Another piece is here. Hmm."

A presence rushed toward the town with great speed. "And now, who could that be?"

Just then, two cars swerved and collided. The drivers climbed out and stood bewildered, wondering what had jumped in front of them. Whatever it was, it had moved too quickly for an ordinary person to see.

"Interesting," Atreyu noted as he listened to a monstrous shriek rising in strength, culminating in a clap of thunder and a flash of lightning.

"LILITH!"

"Well, well, what do we have here? It looks like my dear sister forgot a loose end," he grinned. "Yes, I do believe all the pieces are in place now. It's time to start the show."

With that, he vanished, leaving behind only a Cheshire cat smile.

The story continues in Lilah's Guide to Hoyle.

THIS IS BOB

IT WAS AROUND THREE in the afternoon. A man sat at the bar, his head heavy in his hands, broken and at rock bottom. He'd been fired from his job. His wife and kids had been killed a few weeks earlier.

He motioned for another drink.

"I'm going to have to cut you off if you keep drinking at this rate, Bob," the bartender said.

"C'mon, it's been a tough time for me, alright?" Bob knocked the shot back, feeling the sting in his mouth, and waved for another. "Just let me drink. It's all I got left."

The bartender refilled the glass again, shrugged, and walked away.

Thoughts swirled in Bob's head. The alcohol didn't help matters. He found himself playing with the gun in his coat pocket.

Why don't you kill yourself? He heard a voice say. *There's nothing left for you to live for.*

I should. He sniffled, and tears swelled. *There's no reason to exist anymore. Jill and the kids . . .*

The bartender returned with a sigh. "Damn it, Bob, just here." He poured the grieving man another few shots of vodka. "Take this and go to a corner or something. This shit's killing business."

"Hello, Bob."

He turned to the man beside him—a strange pale man in black with a red right hand.

"I believe I have a business proposition for you."

"What do you want, buddy? Can't a guy just be left alone?"

"You may not know me, but I know you," the Man with the Red Right Hand said with a smile. "And as a matter of fact, I just happen to have a job for you. You've got all the tools to do it, too."

Bob wiped his eyes with a crumpled napkin and gulped down the vodka. "What do you need me to do?"

"Ah, it's nothing that exciting. Just scaring a girl."⸙

Read about Bob and his story in This is Bob: A Guide to Not Dying (Mostly).
You can scan this QR Code.

Look for the dark humor novel *This is Bob: A Guide to Not Dying (Mostly)*, available along with other titles.▯

Book One in the Willborne Saga.

Visit www.abnormalpublishing.com for free stories, information, and more.

Scan this QR Code for *This is Bob: A Guide to Not Dying (Mostly)*.

Acknowledgements

Thanks to my friends and family for your ongoing support.

I want to thank the members of Morphine (rest in peace, Mark Sandman and Billy Conway) for their incredible music. We truly appreciate it. Thanks also to Buckethead and many others for their amazing tunes. A special shoutout to Ghost, Priest, Magna Carta Cartel, Avatar, Volbeat, Gojira, Gothminister, and Night Club. Much love to you all!

Blizzard Entertainment for *World of Warcraft* and my *World of Warcraft* friends on the US server Aegwynn and in the Horde Guild, Revolt: you're all demoted to "Village Bicycle." To my friends in the guild Reboot on US-Illidan: please post more dank memes.

With love,

Sincados

Finally, to *you*, our lovely readers.

See you next time. . .

ABOUT THE AUTHORS

Robert J. McCartney is the author behind *This is Bob* and the ongoing **Willborne Saga**, which includes *Requiem for Lilith* and *Lilah's Guide to Hoyle*. He writes strange and human stories that explore identity, autonomy, and the will to defy fate—often wrapped in dark humor, dream logic, or emotional gut punches.

He lives in Tennessee with his wife, their two children, and an ever-growing backlog of games. When he's not writing or working under his independent label, A.B.Normal Publishing and Media Group, he's probably logged into *World of Warcraft* or plotting the next chapter in his ever-expanding universe.

He also writes an ongoing web series called *The Diary of the Wasteland Bear God*. To read more about Robert's worlds—or to reach out—visit www.abnormalpublishing.com.

Albert J. Debusschere III resides in Michigan. He likes to write, make, and play music, and ponder society and the nature of the universe.

www.ingramcontent.com/pod-product-compliance
Lightning Source LLC
Chambersburg PA
CBHW030235180626
46810CB00008B/3136